Peirene

MARIE SIZUN

*TRANSLATED FROM THE
FRENCH BY ADRIANA HUNTER*

Le Père
de la petite

AUTHOR

Marie Sizun is a prize-winning French author. She was born in 1940 and has taught literature in Paris, Germany and Belgium. She now lives in Paris. Marie Sizun has published seven novels and a memoir. She wrote her first novel, *Her Father's Daughter*, at the age of 65. The book was long-listed for the Prix Femina.

TRANSLATOR

Adriana Hunter has translated over 50 books from French, including works by Agnès Desarthe, Véronique Ovaldé and Hervé Le Tellier. She has translated three previous titles for Peirene: *Beside the Sea* by Véronique Olmi, for which she won the 2011 Scott Moncrieff Prize, *Under the Tripoli Sky* by Kamal Ben Hameda and *Reader for Hire* by Raymond Jean. Adriana has been short-listed twice for the *Independent* Foreign Fiction Prize.

MEIKE ZIERVOGEL
PEIRENE PRESS

This is a poetic story about a girl's love for her father. Told from the girl's perspective, but with the clarity of an adult's mind, we experience her desire to be noticed by the first man in her life. A rare examination of the bonds and boundaries between father and daughter.

First published in Great Britain in 2016 by
Peirene Press Ltd
17 Cheverton Road
London N19 3BB
www.peirenepress.com

First published under the original French-language title *Le Père de la petite* in 2005 by Éditions Arléa, Paris

ISBN 978-1-908670-28-1

Designed by Sacha Davison Lunt
Photographic image by Fabrice Strippoli/Millennium Images, UK
Typeset by Tetragon, London
Printed and bound by T J International, Padstow, Cornwall

This book is supported by the Institut français (Royaume-Uni) as part of the Burgess programme (www.frenchbooknews.com)

INSTITUT
FRANÇAIS
ROYAUME-UNI

Peirene

MARIE SIZUN

TRANSLATED FROM THE
FRENCH BY ADRIANA HUNTER

Her
Father's
Daughter

It's a winter's afternoon in the kitchen of the apartment. They're both there, the mother standing doing her ironing, a tall figure, and beside her the little girl, sitting in her special child's chair. They're not talking at the moment. The child is thinking about what her mother has just said. On the radio a few minutes ago there was some news, news about the war, as usual. When the announcement ended, her mother switched off the radio and, still ironing, said something like 'Your poor little daddy'… or perhaps 'When your poor little daddy comes home'… Offhand. Just like that.

Yes, those were the words she used, not really said to the child, no, but more as if she were talking to herself, pressing the iron slightly more firmly onto the damp linen, and it made the hissing sound swathed in steam that always delights the child. She would normally be enjoying this peaceful moment spent with her mother, in the small kitchen warmed by the heat of her ironing. But right there, in what her mother said, in those words, something loomed before her, something quite new.

Something intruded into the intimate, familiar world of the kitchen. Something the child perceives as a threat. *When. Comes home.*

Behind her, on the end of the shelf, stands the old black radio, and just before her mother turned the knob it was from here that the peculiar man's voice spoke, sounding solemn and metallic, so different from the soft, lilting, almost whispered voice of the child's mother. The voice of spoken news. The child knows it. The voice that talks about the war. The child understands. Her mother has explained. Has told her she has a father who's fighting this war. Or rather he's a prisoner, somewhere far, far away. A father she's never seen, except in photos.

One thing she doesn't understand is that her mother always refers to him as *your little daddy*. But the man she's seen in photographs looks quite tall, he looks a bit like the man at the dairy, or the pork butcher, a bit younger perhaps, not so ugly. Her mother sometimes cries when she talks about him, especially recently. The child doesn't like that. She loathes these tears that give her mother a red nose, puffy eyes and a twisted mouth.

This time her mother didn't cry. She simply looked back down at her ironing, with a big lock of hair hiding her eyes and her mouth, as she said quietly, 'When your little daddy comes home.' Or was it 'When he comes back…'?

Then the child suddenly asks, 'Is he coming back? Why?'

'Why?'

The mother's eyes alight on the child, her expression filled with astonishment and something not unlike pain, and the child gauges all the oddness of that expression. Her mother has carried on ironing and is no longer looking at the child as she says, 'Well, because the war's going to end, my darling. You heard what they said on the radio. All the prisoners are coming home, and your father along with them.'

That's all. The child and her mother fall silent.

There's a big black fly crawling slowly over the yellow and white tiles of the kitchen floor. The child stares, watching its progress. The only thing she can see now is this fly. This big black fly. Nothing but this fly.

'When?' the child asks eventually.

'They don't know. The Germans are already leaving. Soon, probably. Very soon.'

Silence again. The mother and child don't look at each other, each lost in her own thoughts. They're surrounded once again by the warmth of the kitchen, of their familiar world, where everything seems to be in its proper place, the small green cast-iron oven perched on its cabriole-legged stand, the yellow diamonds of the tiled floor, the huge dark stone sink where they wash themselves and the dishes, the shelves and the radio with its curved corners, and the pine table where they have their meals.

The child can't imagine how a man like the butcher or the dairyman could barge in on this, in this very kitchen, in this life of theirs, the life of this mother and her child, this particular life.

'There isn't room here,' she says.

The mother gives her that funny look again, slow, unreadable, secret.

'Don't be silly, my darling, there's plenty of room. We lived here all right before you were born, and we were very happy.'

And yet, as she says these words, happy is the last thing the mother seems to be.

The child doesn't say anything else. It feels to her as if all of a sudden, mysteriously, the world has changed.

She's called France, the child is, France like the country. But no one remembers that now. No one ever calls her by that name, even though it was chosen, duty-bound by the war. They just call her 'the child', that's enough. As for calling her name to summon her, to make her come back, that never happens: the child is always there, close by, under her mother's feet, or consumed with waiting for her. Sometimes, though, her mother gently calls her 'darling', 'my darling', and it's not a summons but a tender form of address. She doesn't pronounce her actual name. Doesn't use it. It's only on paper.

France. Like the country. This name she was given must be something her father decided, with a hint of patriotism, when he was setting off to war. The mother agreed to it, at the time. Now she's forgotten. Doesn't really like the name. So it's a name that doesn't exist. France doesn't exist. The child is quite simply the child. Her mother's child. For now it works. She's only four and a half.

Of the outside world, the child still knows pretty much nothing. And very little about this war going on around them, her and her mother, so intimately and yet so mysteriously, this war which is detaining a father she's never met, this distant and apparently dreadful war. All the child knows of the war is the incomprehensible iron-like voice talking about it on the radio. The opaque comments her mother sometimes makes about it. That's all.

The war, as far as the child is concerned, her personal war, the one she knows, is the shriek of air-raid warnings over Paris, the piercing siren sounds, their sad wails that make everyone scurry for shelter in the Métro and then, deep underground, they stay and wait, until another siren tells them to go home. The war is the sudden emptiness of the next-door apartment, the absence of the Lévys, whose children used to play with her. Led away one morning by shouting policemen. Because of the war, is all her mother said. And it's frightening now walking past that mute doorway. The war is also the strange blue-black paint daubed over all the windows in the stairwell, so the planes dropping bombs can't see our lights at night, apparently. That bluish half-light on the stairs fills your head with dreams and fears.

The restrictions, the ration tickets for food, the queues outside shops, all the things discussed by grown-ups, by women in their building talking among themselves, that's the war too, the child knows it is, but it doesn't really affect her. In fact she loves it when gas and electricity cuts sometimes mean her mother has to cook on a spirit stove which she painstakingly sets up on their little balcony.

And also the war means having those people dotted about the streets, those disturbing, booted characters dressed in dark green, people you have to hurry past, my darling, her mother says, and not say a word. They're frightening and yet, or perhaps precisely because they are, the child thinks they're beautiful.

Lastly, the war was those funny letters on shiny paper, folded into envelope shapes and covered with a filigree of different postmarks in green, red and black, letters her mother received from the prison camp. Before. Letters from her husband. There haven't been any for a long time.

She's never left Paris, the child hasn't, except for once, about a year earlier, when she was three, for a holiday in Normandy with her mother and her grandmother: there was nothing left to eat in the city so, because of the child, we just had to leave, her mother says when she mentions the trip to neighbours. For a few months they lived in an old house on the banks of the Seine, a house surrounded by a garden, which the child remembers with a sense of wonderment loaded with mystery. She can still picture the splash of colour of a red-flowered plant, fuchsias, her mother said; she recalls the smell of leaves and branches being burned outside, the crackle of the flames; she remembers the peppery smell of washing being boiled on a stove in the garden; the creak of a pump with a handle that you cranked to produce a bubbling gush of sparkling water. She remembers other things too, strange things, but she's been told she was dreaming, and her mother and grandmother have forbidden her to talk about them, to *talk nonsense*.

Of Paris, the child knows only the streets and shops in her neighbourhood. The rue Amelot. The shops on the rue de Bretagne. She almost always goes with her mother to do the shopping. At least for food shopping. She also knows the square where her mother goes and sits on a bench to read or chat to people while she, the child, pretends to play in the sandpit. She hates the place, the sand, how aggressive the other children are, her mother's gossipy conversations.

What she knows well, what she likes, is the apartment, their apartment, her mother's and hers, those two rooms and that kitchen, where they've always lived, she and her mother. Their home.

In one room there's a double bed, which belonged to her parents. Her mother sleeps in it alone now, and has done for five years; the child's bed is in the other room, which is actually a dining room, one they use when anyone comes: and that means her grandmother, because there aren't really any other visitors. The grandmother is a seamstress. She used to have a little shop that did quite well before the war. Now she has almost no work at all. So she comes over nearly every day to help her daughter with the housework and the cooking. Sometimes she minds the child if the mother goes out. But she's never lived with them – except during that time in Normandy; she lives in another part of the city, a long way away, near Alésia Métro station. The child and her mother never go there, to the dismal little house on the rue Bezout. A house that matches the grandmother. The child doesn't much like this grey, self-effacing woman who only pretends to be strict. The child and her mother find her boring. The child and her mother love nothing more than having fun. Laughing together. Even if sometimes the mother is overcome with sadness and cries in that terrifying way or, and this is worse, stops talking altogether. Is suddenly reduced to stubborn, incomprehensible silence.

The child's real universe, her entire world and the only imaginable world, is her mother.

Of her mother, the child knows everything – or believes she does. She knows her morning face and her evening face, the smell of her skin and of her hair, how gentle her hands are, how warm her breasts, how soft her tummy. She can identify the different intonations of her voice when she's sad, when she's cheerful, when she's singing or when she's telling stories, or when she chatters about things the child doesn't always understand.

Her mother is beautiful. With an obvious enough beauty for people to turn and look at her in the street. And the child is fascinated by the power of this beauty.

She recognizes by touch, by sight and by smell the short mop of the thick, curly black hair around her mother's face, a face which is always rather pale, its pallor broken by the dazzling red of her lipsticked mouth and the dark agile gleam in her eyes.

She knows and loves, with such a love, the great warm body against which she can snuggle at any time of day. She loves every one of the dresses, even the plainest, that her mother wears, their textures, their smells. She loves her shoes. She loves the way she walks. The way she moves her hands. Her voice. Everything.

She particularly loves the moment every morning when her mother stands in front of the open wardrobe in her slip and asks, 'Tell me, my darling. What can I wear today? What would you advise?'

And the child, earnestly, makes her choice. The mother, almost always, complies. So the child feels she has partly created her mother; that she belongs to her all the more, to her, the child.

And yet something else the child knows about her mother is her absence. The distress this absence produces in her. Sometimes the mother disappears. Goes out. She goes shopping in town. Take me with you, please, says the child. No, that's not possible, don't be silly, I'll be back soon. The child sobs, screams, suffocates, penned in by the bars of her cot when she was younger. The mother has already walked away, intransigent. She has left an old handbag full of small objects in the cot, to keep the child occupied.

Left alone, the child calms down, empties the contents of the bag onto the bedspread and then studies each item at length and in detail: a tube of lipstick, a notebook, a pencil, a bracelet, a hankie, all things that refer back to her mother, that tell stories. Eventually – much, much later, it seems to her – she hears the sound of a key in the lock: her mother is home. The child is so bursting with happiness that her voice is strangulated as she calls, as she cries out, in her frantic longing to see her mother, straight away, quicker, now. The mother laughs. Shush now, shush, she says, putting her hat and bag down on a sideboard, you dotty little thing! I can't hear myself think in here now!

What the child hears is life coming back, the movement, music and fragrance of life coming home.

The child is lifted out of her prison bed: she's on her mother's lap, she's reunited with her mother's smell and her warmth, she'd like to become a part of the mother's body, to hold her so close and so hard that she can never go away again. Ever.

And it's this secret, intimate world, their world for just the two of them, that the child can suddenly feel slipping away.

Your father's coming home. Those words. Now out in the open. Like a threat.

The war had already started when the child was born and he, her father, was very soon captured, a prisoner, sent far away, 'to eastern Prussia', the mother says, when she occasionally tries to explain things to the child. Then she takes out the photos, shows the child letters, the letters from earlier times, when people still received mail, those strange shiny rectangles of white paper, with postmarks from the Stalags. She cries a little every time. The child doesn't much like these episodes.

What is a father? The notion of fatherhood is beyond the child. And how could it not be? Fathers, these days, are pretty thin on the ground. There was the Lévy children's father, but they didn't see him much. The child has almost forgotten him now. The few other children in the building, the concierge's daughter, for example, don't have one: he's a prisoner, or dead, like the father of the two boys on the first floor. Even the child's mother is fatherless: the grandmother's husband is someone they never knew.

Fathers are found in fairy tales, and they're always slightly unreal and not very kind. Or else they're dead, distant, weak, and much less interesting than their daughters and their sons, who are brimming with courage, spirit and good looks.

And then there are animal stories in the children's books that the child leafs through, looking at the pictures while the mother reads the words out to her: the generations are respected and fathers, be they dogs, horses or bears, are clearly represented; like in the story of 'Goldilocks and the Three Bears', which keeps bombarding you with the triad of Daddy Bear, Mummy Bear and Baby Bear until you've completely understood, little children, that a normal family is made up of a father, a mother and a child. But the child isn't at all convinced. She still thinks Daddy Bear comes across as incongruous in the story, too heavy, too big.

Of course you can see images of human fathers, proper, realistic, instructive pictures of fathers, in advertising posters in the streets and the Métro. Those big pictures pasted onto the walls of Métro stations, showing smiling families sitting at a table together around a pot of hearty soup or a semolina pudding, which the child happens to loathe. And in the middle, tall, well dressed, closely shaven and smiling twice as much, is the father. An enigma.

When she looks at the photographs of her own father – casually, slightly at arm's length, as if almost afraid of burning her fingers – she gets only a vague impression of him. These photos are images of a past she doesn't know, of no importance to her. Her mother perseveres, puts a wedding photo in the child's hand: in it she, the mother, is in a white dress on the arm of a smiling young man, by the door of a church; and look, my darling, he's so handsome in this one, when the child sees only a soldier in uniform, a stranger with empty eyes; or this one then, one the mother's just found of a couple, sweethearts dancing at a party, and the young woman is her mother, the young man, her father. But I can't really see, says the child.

On the other hand, the one in which you can see him best, really 'him', is the larger photograph under glass that always stands on the sideboard in the dining room, a photograph devoted entirely to his face.

A picture she no longer even notices because it's there before her eyes every day.

And ever since those words evoking a possible return were spoken, those terribly peculiar and disturbing words, it is this portrait that the child has taken to studying surreptitiously every time she passes it. Scrutinizing it in great detail when she is alone. The image of the stranger who's going to come here, to live here with her mother and her, no one knows when, but soon.

She thinks he looks sad and stern. And yet he doesn't look old. It's his eyes that worry the child, eyes loaded with unknown thoughts, eyes that have never seen her, the child, eyes that aren't looking at her either, but are staring past her at something else, someone else. It's this stranger's stare that frightens her.

Your father's coming home. As if she were already subjected to that stare.

In the meantime, the child tries to behave as if nothing has changed. She plays under the dining-room table; you can't see the picture from there. She runs through the apartment singing at the top of her lungs. She uses any excuse to throw her arms around her mother's neck and kiss her dementedly.

'The child's becoming completely insufferable,' the grandmother says.

The mother smiles without a word, her pretty, sad smile that seems to understand everything.

The grandmother says the child is badly brought up. In fact the child hasn't been brought up at all: because, with her mother's backing, under her mother's adoring eye, she does almost whatever she wants, says what she wants and eats what she wants when she wants. The child is well aware that the mother and grandmother disagree on the subject; but it's the mother who decides, who has the last word, and the grandmother can only bow her head with a sigh; the child knows this, listening inquisitively to their conversations, or at least what she understands of them.

As it happens, she abuses this freedom with relative restraint. What does she do? She only draws a little bit on the walls, the grey walls of their small apartment, with her colouring pencils; she fills the pages of the books she finds with mysterious symbols that appeal to her. She likes bringing these dead pages to life. She sings too, very loudly, at any time of day, tunes she has invented, with a warlike feel, particularly if her mother stops paying attention to her, to speak to the grandmother, for example. Then the child makes sure she's listened to. Demands it.

The child is temperamental, 'spoilt', in the grandmother's words. She refuses to eat things she doesn't like, particularly the little meals put together by the grandmother using whatever's available, whatever the war has left them: cod stew, Jerusalem artichokes, semolina in milk.

When the fancy takes her, the child gets down from the table without a word and goes off to play. Which makes her mother laugh.

'Leave her, just leave her,' the mother says in reply to the old lady's protests. 'If only *I'd* had such freedom as a child…'

She laughs to see the child so happy, watches her go with adoring eyes.

'You're my darling, aren't you?' she calls after her. And the child, caressed by her gaze, turns round without uttering a word, agrees with a conspiratorial smile, rapturously happy.

The child doesn't like her grandmother. Not at all. She doesn't like that grey hair, that tight bun at the nape of the grandmother's neck, those eyes which are such a pale blue they look transparent, those cool, drooping white cheeks, that flat chest, that immutable sadness, a sadness which weighs down on her old shoulders and diffuses a veil of gloom and boredom. The child doesn't like the insipid smell of the old woman. She doesn't like the hushed, monotonous, sensible voice, which never has any spark, any gusto. She doesn't like the touch of the permanently icy hands when the grandmother's making a dress for the child and wants to try it on her (how the child shies away then, how she screams that she's afraid of the pins). And most of all the child doesn't like the private conversations her grandmother has with the mother, her own mother, the child's, her property, and she can't see how her mother can conceivably be this woman's daughter. She hates the old woman's love for her daughter, the demonstrations of affection, kisses, gestures, words. She particularly loathes the name she calls her, that pet name, Li, for Liliane. Sometimes, and this is the worst of it, the grandmother even says, 'Li, my child.' *She* is the child, and no one else, and her mother is Mummy. No other names. The child thinks there's something odd, inappropriate, about any familiarity between the two women, anything that implies a special connection between them. And specifically, recently, the conversations from which she, the child, is excluded.

But what she especially hates, what she can't abide, is that her grandmother is a liar. Her grandmother lied to her once, and this the child has never forgotten.

The mother lied too that time. But that doesn't matter. It's not the same. The child doesn't resent her mother for it.

It feels like a long time ago. She can't really tell any more. It was in the past. They don't talk about it now. *We're not allowed to talk about it.*

It was an event the child didn't understand. Something very peculiar. That she's never managed to clarify. She still thinks about it sometimes. She settles under the dining-room table and wonders about it.

She was lied to once. There was something she'd seen with her own eyes, and was told she hadn't seen. Told she'd dreamed it. That's what her grandmother and her mother said. They lied. But it mustn't be mentioned again. It's completely forbidden. How angry they were, even her mother. They shouted. Forbidden ever to raise the subject again. The only thing forbidden to this child, who usually does as she pleases.

So she thinks about it, all alone, from time to time. Such a strange, muddled memory, but so clear too. You were dreaming, her mother and grandmother said. No, she wasn't dreaming. She knows *it* did exist. But it now feels so long ago. It's true, it is a bit like a dream.

The thing happened during that glorious, unusual trip to Normandy with her mother and grandmother, an almost make-believe trip – When? How long ago? The child doesn't know, doesn't yet have a sense of duration, dates, calendars – a trip filled with indistinct images, all the more exquisite for their volatility, a garden in the rain, the red splash of tear-shaped flowers, smells of woodsmoke.

It was right in the middle of this wonderful trip that the peculiar scene appeared, incomprehensible and yet infinitely pleasurable, like every other part of it, this would even be its crowning moment, if they hadn't told her it never happened and that they didn't want to hear it mentioned.

It's like a dream, *but it isn't a dream*.

She goes with her grandmother to visit the mother, who, rather surprisingly, is in hospital, in a white room, in a white bed, but she isn't ill, she's smiling. They sit the child down next to the bed, on a chair, beside her grandmother, who's also on a chair. All at once the door opens: in comes a nurse, carrying a snugly swaddled baby, which she hands to the mother; then, noticing the child, the nurse smiles at her, lifts her nimbly over the bed so she has a better view, and tells her to *look how pretty her little sister is. They're going to have a lot of fun together, aren't they.*

Those words. And then the nurse leaves.

Just for a moment the child saw, wrapped in a blanket, the crumpled red face of a sleeping baby.

Astonishment. Momentary rapturous delight.

But after that, nothing. Afterwards, there's nothing. The child remembers nothing. How her mother behaved, or her grandmother, what they did and said.

Her memories pick up with the journey back to the house in Normandy, the child accompanied only by her grandmother. Her mother stayed in hospital.

'And the baby?' the child asks. 'When's she coming? When?'

Silence. The child continues obstinately.

'When's *my little sister* coming back with Mummy?' she keeps saying.

And from the grandmother: 'What are you talking about? You've got things wrong. You don't have a little sister. The nurse made a mistake. But your mummy's coming back, *she's* coming back. Soon. She's been a bit ill, that's all.'

Fury from the child, who ploughs on, incredulous. Protests. Persists. In vain.

When, some time later, the mother returns, alone, without a baby, the child bombards them with questions again, obstinate, sure the grandmother misunderstood, didn't know, was lying. But now her mother too is telling her she's wrong, she dreamed it. The child works herself into a state, stamping her feet with rage and hurt, crying. She knows what she saw, doesn't she?

Loathing her grandmother, who's shaking her head inanely.

Towards her mother, the child feels no anger. Just tremendous surprise. The sadness of not being believed. The disappointment of not understanding.

And eventually the child would calm down. Would forget a bit. Would stop asking questions. Besides, she'll be forbidden to mention the whole episode again.

She does think about it from time to time, though, about this oddity. She doesn't know. She no longer knows.

The child often dreams, and sometimes believes she's living something for real. Her dreams can be so beautiful and so powerful. Like the time when she stepped into an astonishing house made of glass, in the middle of a forest. Those colours, that light, those smells… And then she woke up and there was nothing there, no house of glass, no forest, just the grey dining room where she sleeps. And it was this reality that she couldn't immediately believe.

So when are we living and when are we dreaming?

That's complicated enough already. But the child suspects that grown-ups confuse things on purpose. As her mother and grandmother did, that fateful day, for some obscure reason.

The child is wary of anything that might bring the women closer. Like these recent confabulations, these whispered words, when they think she, the child, can't hear. The mysterious looks they exchange.

This very morning, in fact, the grandmother has just arrived and she's already towing her daughter off towards the window and talking to her in a hushed voice. The mother has that frightened expression the child doesn't like.

The child, who was sitting thinking under the dining-room table, immediately pops out and comes to prowl around them, and the old woman turns to her irritably and shoos her away.

'You again, nosy parker! Run along and play. Leave us alone for a minute.' And as the child doesn't do as she's told… 'Go and play, I said! Oh, honestly. This is all going to change, you'll see. When your father comes home, you'll have to toe the line!'

The mother says nothing. Silent, thoughtful, miles away, not even looking at her child, her daughter. Strangeness surrounds the mother completely.

Furious, the child withdraws to the corridor. There on a chair she finds her grandmother's black overcoat and her handbag. She empties the bag onto the floor. And tramples all over its contents.

What's going on in this house? What's making time drag by so slowly all of a sudden? Why are words spoken so quietly and how come noises are so hushed?

In their grey apartment, where the grandmother is gaining a foothold, now coming every day, it feels as if time has stopped. Weighty, crushing the child who was once so light, so free with her mother, so happy alone with her. The child sang and danced and drew and laughed. And her mother laughed along with her.

Now, though, there's no laughter to be heard.

At the moment the mother and grandmother are conferring, a little way away.

The white faces of worried women. Whisperings. Desultory gestures. Interrupted movements. Waiting. But nothing happens.

The child starts to sing in the silence, but keeps her ears open.

And now, through her singing, she hears perfectly clearly. Those words again. Her father's coming home. Soon. This week. Straight away?

She behaves as if nothing's happened. Carries on singing.

The two women have stopped talking. They're now both gazing at her in silence. For the first time the child thinks they look alike.

Something not unlike fear has come into the room.

Days of this peculiar waiting go by. Nothing happens, but you can feel that everything's about to change, soon, any minute.

This time they explain to the child more clearly that the war isn't yet completely over, but that her father, who's ill, will be coming home, in a special convoy, with other prisoners who are also ill.

'What's wrong with him?'

The mother says she doesn't really know. All she's received is an official document. No direct news. No letter from the father. Apparently he's had pneumonia; apparently his nerves aren't good either. That's all she knows. The army have told her he's being sent home urgently. That was all.

'When's he coming back?'

'Soon, my darling, soon.'

'When?'

The child would find out nothing else today. But she would ask plenty more questions. In vain.

She wanders around her little domain, which has

become slightly unfamiliar, draws half-heartedly on her favourite wall, watches what's going on around her, listens, lurks, alert to anything that might supply an answer to her concerns.

'Mummy?'

'What, my darling?'

'No, nothing...'

How pale she is, her mother, how pretty she is as she studies herself in the mirror now, with that anxious, darting expression, contemplating an eyebrow with a delicate tilt of her head, lifting a lock of hair with one finger.

'Wait, Mummy, I'll brush your hair,' the child says.

She fetches a hairbrush and a comb, makes her mother sit on the edge of the bed, then climbs up behind her and starts untangling her curly hair, slowly, tenderly. Then, abandoning the brush, she dives her little hands voluptuously into that black mane, again and again.

In the end she puts her arms around her mother's neck, presses her face to the nape and asks very softly, 'Will you still love me?'

'You dotty little thing! Of course I'll still love you!'

'More than him?'

'Who do you mean, him?'

The mother's momentarily forgotten, then understands.

'You mean your daddy?... But it's not the same. You're a little girl...'

'But even so… Will you love me more than him?'
Why does the mother now look so sad, so tired?
'If you like, yes. I'll love you more than him.'
The child is satisfied with this assertion, for now.

At last the evening comes when, as she puts her to bed, the mother kisses her child in a ceremonious way. Looks at her. Says nothing. This time, the child thinks, her heart beating hard, she's going to tell me. She's going to tell me now. *He's coming.*

And sure enough, that's what this is about. The mother tells the child that a convoy of prisoners has reached Paris, that her father is in hospital and they'll go to see him tomorrow. Tomorrow morning.

The child says nothing, gripped by the enormity of this news, however anticipated it was, terrified by the imminence of things. She fiddles agitatedly with her mother's hand, a limp, passive white hand. She tries with all her might to picture what's about to happen. She doesn't hear what her mother's saying, in her soft voice, leaning over her, like when she tries to get her to sleep, speaking right up close to her. She can't see her face, her eyes, just her cheeks, the grain of the skin on her cheeks, and those cheeks suddenly look very full to her, odd. She touches them so her fingers can re-establish the soft feel of them, the truth of them.

The mother and child stay like that in silence.

'Are you pleased, my darling?' the mother asks eventually. 'You're going to see your little daddy tomorrow.'

'He's not little,' the child protests, her words whispered.

'Yes he is, my darling, it's an expression, you'll see how young and kind he is…'

The child grabs her mother by the neck and, still speaking softly, asks whether just this evening she can sleep with her in the big bed where very soon, she knows, someone else will lie.

Granted. The mother takes the child through to her room, the child who will sleep, right through till morning, curled up against her mother.

And now, this morning, this March morning, here they are running, the mother and the child, running towards the Métro station. They're off to see the father. This experience is happening at last. This adventure.

With one hand the mother keeps hold of the child, with the other she's carrying a big box from Printemps department store, and it keeps bashing against her legs. Inside it there are civilian clothes for her husband, clothes which, till now, were stowed away in the wardrobe, clothes the child has never seen.

She herself, the child, has been dressed very carefully. She's been put into her prettiest dress, the green velvet one with smocking and a lace collar. An attempt has been made to curl her hair, but it didn't work. Anyway, she's wearing shoes of black patent leather and white ankle socks.

As for her mother, she's looking very pretty, she's done her make-up beautifully, done her hair beautifully, and she's dug out her navy-blue jacket and a white blouse. The child preferred the low-cut red dress, but the mother didn't want that. Nevertheless, the result is lovely, and the child told her mother so, which seemed to please her.

They're walking as quickly as they can, because they're now late. Visiting time is eleven o'clock, we'll never get there, says the mother. Flights of stairs in the Métro station at top speed.

Waiting on the platform with her mother, holding her mother's hand, the child sees the huge underground train arriving, its carriages following the curve of the tunnel as it draws in to the station. Strangely, this is the detail she will remember from that day, the image of those carriages solemnly cornering behind the leading car. The image of her anguish.

Now, sitting facing one another as they travel towards the unknown, the child and her mother look at each other. They're emotional, for different reasons, each in her own way, each lost in her own thoughts. Soon the child turns away towards the window and, without seeing it, gazes at the grey walls of the tunnel on which, here and there, the bright colours of an advertising hoarding blaze at her – letters spelling out in yellow and blue *Dubo-Dubon-Dubonnet*, or the jolly face and bouncy white body of the Michelin Man, a funny figure who used to make her laugh. But today she doesn't even look at him.

'Only five more stops,' her mother whispers. She's holding the Printemps box on her lap, and the child notices that her hands are shaking.

And now all of a sudden the lights have gone out and, with a lurch that piles the standing passengers into each other, the train stops abruptly. A long screech, then nothing. They're in total darkness. Engine off.

At first there's a heavy silence, then exclamations came from every direction in the dark; eventually there's a hubbub of voices in every direction. Someone's shouting that there must be bombing overhead. Someone else mentions a strike.

'Oh, God,' mutters the mother, 'and we're already so late!'

A voice comes through a loudspeaker, asking the passengers to stay calm.

A woman screams that she wants to get off.

The mother drops the box to the floor and takes the child on her lap.

The child, just for a moment, is filled with irrational hope: there in the dark, as she huddles against her mother, she thinks something extraordinary is happening and that it might spare her from going to see her father.

But then a ghostly conductor appears with a lamp in his hand: ladies and gentlemen, it's just a power cut. The passengers will have to get to the next station on foot, walking over the ballast, along the tunnel.

Everyone's shouting. People lunge for the doors in the half-dark.

The child will always remember that precise moment, that stampede for the doors, how strange it was climbing down from the carriage onto the ballast, such a long way down, it seemed to her, in the dark tunnel: people help her mother get down with her box, while she, the child, is carried and handed to her mother.

The memory stops there. With that extraordinary hope, quickly shattered, that nothing's happening. That she could avoid the father. And then this descent in the dark.

Of walking over the stones she has no recollection at all, nor of reaching the next stop, emerging from the Métro station, seeing daylight again, nor the long trek through the streets all the way to the hospital – because it turns out that they do have to go there. Too tired, too emotional perhaps. Did her mother carry her, in one arm, with the box in the other?

The child reduced to such a helplessly little child again.

It is probably late, too late perhaps, when they reach the hospital. He must be so desperate to see us, says the mother, hurry up, and now the child is trotting along, clinging to her mother while she, the mother, still clutches the Printemps box, which is also looking pretty tired. The mother is rather flushed, her hair slightly awry, the child's shoes no longer shine.

They are directed to a room on an upper floor, at the end of a corridor with doors to other rooms, where the child glimpses rows of beds and men's faces. Rows and rows of beds and faces. It could just as easily be here, this one, now, but it's never this one. There are still more. The father could be in any one of these rooms, he could be any one of these men. The father could be anybody.

At last they really are there, this is the right room, the one with the right number over it, the one where they should find the right father.

All nerves, the mother and child step hand in hand into the large white room filled with the harsh light of tall parallel windows to the right and left towering over two rows of beds, lots of beds, so many beds, the full length of the room. And on every bed a man, sitting or lying, awake or asleep, young or old, it depends, they come in every variety here. Which one's her father? This one or that one? The child will soon know. And now she's the one dragging her mother, who's become peculiarly heavy. The child thinks she'll be able to identify him without any help, all by herself. As she walks past these men in their beds, she stares at them like an inspector: it's not this fat man sitting here, stooped, slightly balding, playing cards with a neighbour, not the neighbour either, such an old man; nor this tall, thin man with dishevelled black hair, reading his newspaper; or this one who's so ill all he can do is lie there with his eyes closed like a corpse; could it be this young man smiling up into her eyes?

But her mother has stopped beside a bed in the other row, a bed that, in her speculations about possible fathers, the child didn't notice: in it is a very thin man with a gaunt face, not very old, but not young either; he's sitting up in bed looking at them with a peculiar smile, a slightly nervous smile. The child eventually recognizes the face from the photographs. There. It's him. It's her father. And yet it's someone else.

The child is out of her depths in this mystery.

She's being spoken to. She doesn't hear. Curiously, she's the one the stranger speaks to first, his words disconcertingly formal. But what it is he's saying, she doesn't grasp. The words, the voice, the tone are not things she knows. Not things she recognizes. Too unfamiliar.

'Good afternoon, young lady... Hello, France!' says the man who is her father, while, to the child's horror, one of his hands pulls the mother close to him, quite simply brings her to him, sits her down on the edge of the bed, right beside him, puts an arm round her, without speaking to her, and the mother lets her head drop onto that shoulder without speaking either, and she buries her face in it, and the child sees that her eyes are full of tears. But it's all happening so quickly now that the child can't see or understand everything. Just details.

'You're very pretty, Miss France,' the man goes on, hugging his wife to him, but still keeping his words for the child standing beside the bed, the child who doesn't know what to do and looks down at her socks, now grey with dust.

Is it the mismatch between what he's doing and what he's saying, what he's doing addressed to the mother and what he's saying addressed to her, the daughter? Unsettled, the child stays silent, her head still obstinately lowered.

'I'm delighted to meet you...' the unfamiliar voice goes on, with the same affectation of formality, the same earnest kindliness.

'Come on, my darling,' the mother says through her tears – yes, she's really crying properly now – 'give your daddy a kiss, then!'

The child doesn't move.

The man leans towards her and kisses her. Looks at her. The child feels awkward at the touch of him. His eyes on her. She's still made of stone. But he's already sitting back up.

'You're not very talkative, young lady. So, you see, because I'm of no interest to you, I'm going to pay a bit more attention to another pretty lady,' he says with a smile.

And now he's kissing the child's mother, on the mouth this time, slowly, and, surprised and embarrassed, the child looks away.

'Why don't you sit her on the bed?' the husband says to his wife.

The child is put on the bed, perched at the foot, a little way away from the couple.

'Give her my box of pipes,' he says next, indicating something on the bedside table, 'to keep her busy…'

The mother hands the child a small painted wooden box.

Sitting motionless, the child focuses all her attention on the lid, which is decorated with a colourful picture of a horseman on a galloping white steed. She can see nothing except this image now, shuts herself away in mindlessly contemplating it, far removed from these two people kissing and talking in hushed tones so close by. On and on go their hushed tones. Their gazing.

Inside the child's head, in her body, something turns to ice.

*

How long will this performance last? The child now feels as if time, which went by so swiftly earlier, has stopped, as if she's been here for hours, sitting on the end of this bed. She's been forgotten. They don't see her. She's disappeared. She's not in this world.

She opens the box she's been lent. The acrid smell of tobacco, violently unfamiliar to the child. Inside are two small pipes, one made of wood; the other has a white porcelain bowl with decorative painting. A little picture in colour: against a wooded background, huntsmen in strange clothes.

Paralysed in a sort of torpor, the child longs only to be delivered, for them to leave.

Apparently the man who is her father won't be coming home with them today. He needs to rest a little longer.

Of the journey home alone with her mother, the child will remember nothing.

No memories either of the days immediately after that first meeting. A black hole. An absence. As if none of it existed. As if, after that hospital visit, she abstained from looking, thinking or even feeling, or as if she had forgotten to do these things. Just got through this time, slept through this time, an interlude.

What did the mother and child say to each other over those last few days spent alone? What questions did the child ponder, what thoughts did she churn over? There's no knowing.

'The child's going soft in the head,' concluded the grandmother when the child failed to respond to a request she'd made for the third time.

The child is dreaming. It's as if she's asleep on her feet.

One day – it may have been one evening – the father eventually came home. For real this time. He came home to the apartment, all on his own, by surprise, sooner than expected. The doctors must have thought he was better.

The child was looking at some pictures when she heard the doorbell ring. Her mother, who went to open the door, let out a scream. When the child came to see what was going on, she found her parents in each other's arms. The thin man and her mother. They hadn't moved from the landing. Then the child was noticed, standing beside them, in silence. The husband stepped away from his wife for a moment to take the child in his arms and kiss her. He picked her up and kissed her. What he said, no one remembers, but it was nice. He didn't say 'young lady' this time. Didn't use that urbane tone of voice. And then he put the child down again and turned back to the mother.

The child was put to bed earlier than usual that evening.

When she woke the next morning, she'd sort of forgotten. She wanted to go and see her mother as usual, but when she opened the door to her bedroom, she remembered things: there in the double bed, still fast asleep, were two people, her mother and someone else. Her father.

The child closed the door again.

So. He was there. She had a father.

A very strange thing for the child, having a father. A father who's there. At home. All the time. Morning, noon and night. He's all you can hear now. And that smell's everywhere, the peculiar smell of that wooden box from the first day, the smell of tobacco, and of the pipe he smokes from the moment he wakes up, champing at it the whole time, making his mouth slope slightly to one side.

The child watches him surreptitiously. And the more she studies him, the more surprising she finds him. He no longer looks anything like the photograph which still has pride of place on the sideboard, the picture of the young man who looks so sad and gentle, 'your little daddy', as her mother used to say. You'd think it wasn't the same person, and yet, if you look closely, he's recognizable. But it feels almost as if he's become the father of the sad boy in the photo.

There he is, sitting on the sofa in the dining room, drawing on his pipe with a funny little sucking noise, watching everything with his cold blue eyes, eyes as serious as the words he uses.

There he is, so thin, with his great big legs, and his great big hands with their odd covering of freckles, and the pallor of his long bony face. He does nothing. He stays there, smoking, motionless. He watches. He watches everything. He sees everything.

When he talks it's impossible to tell whether he's angry or joking. His words are always rather knowing, but never the same: gentle one minute, abrupt the next, tender with the mother one minute, formal with the child the next. And then suddenly aggressive. Brutal. Violent.

It's surprising. It's frightening. Sometimes very frightening.

The father is still ill, apparently. It will be a long time before he can go back to work with the insurance company that employed him before the war. The mother whispers in the child's ear that she must be very good, because of daddy's *nerves*, she must *be careful*. What that means, the child will fairly soon come to understand.

The first time her father flew into a rage, she was terrified. Now she knows, but she's still very frightened every time it happens.

The father has sudden, terrible, unpredictable tempers. Lots of things make him angry, big things too complicated for the child – she catches words at random, the war, the camps, the Stalags, the French, the Germans, Pétain, the collaborators, the black market – and others she understands better, more familiar, relating to what's going on here, at home, his home, the father's.

Because this apartment, the mother's and the child's home, is *his*, apparently. And he may well be happy to be reunited with the wife he loves, but he's not at all satisfied with how his household is run, with the mess in the apartment, or more particularly with the terrible way she's been brought up, her, the child. A disaster, he says. He didn't like the graffiti on the walls at all, the father didn't. Li, my darling, how could you put up with it? And even in books! The father can't get over it. And the wailing, the stupid singing? It's unbelievable, says the father. Is she abnormal? And her table manners! And her fussy eating, inconceivable in wartime, unacceptable! Do you understand how it feels for me, my darling, coming back to this after four years in captivity? This? She's spoilt, the child is, completely spoilt.

The child listens, knows perfectly well he's talking about her, doesn't fully understand what she's supposed to have done wrong, but feels uncomfortable. Particularly as the father switches very quickly from the relative gentleness of restrained criticism to fury, firestorms. He shouts and bellows.

My darling, for her part, looks at the floor, contrite, mumbling goodness knows what, meek, almost ashamed. She capitulates, submits, going over to the enemy. All of a sudden the mother no longer champions the child, her child. She's no longer her accomplice, laughing about the grandmother's criticism. The mother is siding with this angry man. Siding with her husband.

*

Everything's different now, the child can certainly see that. He's in charge now. The father. Another life is beginning, with new rules.

So there are some very simple things that now can't happen. Writing on the walls, for example, or in books. Or singing. The first time the child launched, not thinking, into one of her old warrior-like chants, the father appeared from nowhere, yelling that she was splitting his head open, implying she should be quiet. Terrified, the mother intervened, took the child to one side, talking in hushed tones about the father's migraines, his illness, explaining, begging, with the oddest expression on her face. The child is quiet now. She's amazed, but she's quiet.

She doesn't understand what's going on. Can't grasp what they want her to do. What her father wants. She only knows she isn't as she ought to be. That she's a hindrance. A nuisance. Yes, she's a nuisance. And that really is the most difficult thing to accept for someone whose mother used to call her 'my beloved'.

The child can see that, whatever the situation, she's now annoying. She can feel the disapproval in the way her father looks at her, whatever she does, his irritation, an irritation that, she's well aware, could suddenly change to fury. Particularly at mealtimes, when he discovers the full extent of her bad manners, her rudeness.

One of the first images from the early days after the father's homecoming is of the new little family having a meal together. The father is sitting at the table with the two of them, the mother and the child. They now have meals in the dining room, even when the grandmother isn't there. In fact, the old lady very tactfully comes much less frequently, only on Sundays.

There the father is, always in the same place, opposite the mother, sitting very upright, looking worried. He's watching. He notices everything. The child now has to stay seated for the entire meal. No question of getting down to play. The father's face that first time when, halfway through, she tried to slip quietly off her chair! How quickly he put her back in her place! But what he really, really insists on is that she eat everything, absolutely everything on her plate, down to the last mouthful. And without a sound. The father can't bear the sound of chewing. If the child ignores this rule, something terrifying happens. The father goes red, bangs on the table, screams that he was hungry for four whole years, he saw men die, that the very sight of this picky little girl is unbearable, intolerable, scandalous… That her table manners are revolting. That even on the farm, when he was a prisoner… His voice gets extraordinarily loud. He's bellowing. The mother starts to cry. The child shakes.

In a nutshell, the father feels the same as the grandmother: the child's been very badly brought up. But it's not too late. We'll break her in, he says. He's going to do just that.

The child may now have a father but, on the other hand, she might as well no longer have a mother. Because as if by magic her mother is reduced to being a docile wife to her husband, his sweetheart, his servant. Perhaps she no longer has time to look after the child. Perhaps she no longer feels like it. Besides, indications have been made that she should limit her displays of affection towards her daughter, she should stop sitting her on her lap as she used to, and stop using any excuse to address her with that idiotic 'my darling'.

'Her name's France!' the father interjects brusquely whenever this happens.

Should the child try to hug her mother as she used to, with her arms clinging around her neck, it's the mother he takes it out on. And in a fairly abrasive tone of voice. The child's certainly noticed that.

'Stop babying her!' he says. 'She's too big for you to put up with such childish behaviour.'

If the mother protests, weakly, he gets angry. And the room reverberates with the boom of his fearsome voice, which hurts the child as much as if it were addressed to her – true, it is about her he's talking.

And what overwhelms the child far more than her fear of her father is the things she's discovering in her mother: her silence, her weakness, her reticence, her extraordinary resignation, which the child doesn't yet know to describe as cowardice but which she feels is an offence, serious, unforgivable.

And this is why sometimes, when the mother's being scolded by her husband, the child isn't altogether displeased that the mother should be punished indirectly for her betrayal.

The child then slinks slyly off to a corner, under the dining-room table, for example, and gazes blankly into space, waiting for the storm to pass. Her heart beats gently, in a state of fear mixed with something like pleasure.

From the child's point of view, arguments between her father and her mother have another advantage in that, for a time, they suspend any lovey-dovey behaviour. Because that – those kisses, the way they tenderly put their arms around each other and whisper things she can't hear – is something the child doesn't like. Likes less and less.

It is strange for the child to discover disenchantment, jealously. Feelings she couldn't put a name to, but which hurt inside your stomach, and your heart.

The child can see she's no longer the object of her mother's adoration. The loved one is her father. He's called 'darling' now, not her. He's looked at, as she was before, with that tender, slightly anxious expression, not her. He's admired. Not her. Not any more.

As for the stories her mother would read to her, sitting her on her lap, and the invented stories she would tell her at night, speaking so softly in her lilting voice, there are no more of those.

The child's mother has a husband.

When the three of them go out together, the child and her parents, when they go for a walk on a Sunday through the streets in their neighbourhood, and all the way to the Place des Vosges, they make the child walk in front. They follow, with their arms round each other's waists, a pair of lovers, a few paces behind.

At first she didn't understand, accustomed when outside to holding her mother's hand at all times. That was the rule then. It's different now. In fact it's the very opposite.

'Walk ahead, I tell you,' her father kept saying, when she hesitated. 'We won't lose you.'

So she walked along, forging blindly in a straight line, intimidated by her solitude, her awkwardness, her empty hands.

And if she showed signs of slowing down or turning round, her father's voice was there: 'Keep going, don't stop!'

Or perhaps: 'Left, turn left!'

Left, right, what does that mean? The child has no idea. She really hasn't been taught *anything*, her father shouts. Thank goodness he's there. That's all going to change.

The mother smiles at her husband.

The child suddenly hates the pair of them. It occurs to her that she'd like to be lost. Or to lose them.

Will you still love me? More than him?

Liar.

And then came the scene, one mealtime, a repetition of so many others, but more violent and, for the child, a confirmation of her abandonment.

The three of them are sitting at the table, the father and mother facing each other and the child in between. The parents are talking calmly. The child is silent. On her plate there's still a little pile of pasta that she's eyeing anxiously, whitish twirls; they look disgusting, she doesn't think she'll be able to eat them. The father breaks off from the conversation, pins his pale eyes on the child and says simply, 'I'm waiting.'

Feeling sick at the sight of the pasta, the child doesn't move.

Then he roars. He thumps the table with his fist. He shouts. He shouts things that have now become routine for the child but, bellowed like this, they terrify her: what he went through, the cold, the hunger, the sickness. He shouts that he's disgusted by the child's fussiness. He shouts, and every word reverberates, and the table shudders with every blow thumped out in time to his words.

'Oh, darling, come on,' the mother intervenes timidly, sitting motionless on her side of the table.

'Keep out of this, Li, please. France knows very well what she needs to do. Don't you, France? And you're going to do it, aren't you?'

He's dropped his voice. But that's almost worse. The father is now white with anger. His words insidious, demented, incontestable.

The child is quivering with nerves. His voice, his repetitions, his closeness are turning her stomach. She wants to be sick. She wants to cry. But she holds herself back. Making a tremendous effort, she loads her fork once more, puts it into her mouth, almost retching in disgust, and makes herself swallow.

'Again,' says the father. 'You haven't finished.'

The child looks at him, looks at his strange, stony face, briefly meets those unsettlingly pale eyes, those inflexible eyes. Looking at him feels like drowning.

She makes herself swallow, again and again. Swallowing to the death.

Has she finished? No. With her stomach heaving, she can see there's still food on her plate.

And this time, when the voice needles her again, metallic, unbearable, it's too much. The contents of the child's stomach rise up to her mouth, explode, streaming onto the table, between the plates, onto the clean tablecloth, everywhere.

Unacceptable. Disgusting.

The father stands up, turns to the child, who's sitting abjectly on her chair, yanks her violently by one arm and slaps her, once on one side of the face, once on the other.

The mother lets out a scream. But doesn't move. Doesn't speak.

And because the child is now sobbing, gasping helplessly, he opens the door of the apartment and pushes her, choking, onto the landing.

She wails.

'You can come back in when you've calmed down,' her father bellows, before slamming the door behind her.

With all the noise, doors have opened here and there, and are swiftly closed again. Intimidated and ashamed, the child falls silent and, still convulsed by sobs, she goes and sits sniffling in a quiet corner, on a stair. And she waits, filled with loathing, for someone to be good enough to come and get her.

But, interestingly, it's towards her mother – passive, submissive and slightly ridiculous – that all her resentment is directed.

One person who's very happy with the new shape of things is the grandmother. At last a bit of discipline and organization in this house! At last someone's going to teach the child how to behave! At last her little Li has seen sense! The grandmother is all smiles when she comes, all sweetness towards her returning son-in-law, the head of the family. But she manages to be discreet, the grandmother does, she doesn't force herself on them too often.

She comes over for lunch on Sundays. Oh, the satisfaction when the child is brought into line! She smiles at her daughter, smiles at her daughter's husband. Life has gone back to normal. They make a proper family.

Sitting at the table during those long Sunday lunches, the child, who isn't included in the conversation, is at her leisure to watch them, the three of them, the grandmother, the father and the mother. She watches them surreptitiously, pretending she isn't, sneakily, the grandmother says.

The grandmother, triumphant, their guest, in pride of place at the head of the table, her eyes bright, her words honeyed, her every move self-assured.

The father, whom the child now knows, she knows him by heart, but he still astonishes her. She knows the blond, almost white hair cut very short, the very light blue eyes which focus fiercely under the effects of anger, the pale complexion which can flush red or, conversely, go deathly white. She also knows, and dreads, the big hands, which like his arms are smattered with freckles, strong hands resting on either side of his plate when he's calm, hands the child can't take her eyes off. She now recognizes, even from a distance, the smell of tobacco that hovers over them.

When everything's all right, when there's no reason for irritation, the father looks tenderly at his wife, talks softly to her, thoughtfully to the grandmother, and ignores the child. In the event of a problem, if a storm threatens, if a criticism comes to light, the grandmother invariably and with sugary servility takes her son-in-law's side, even going so far as to disagree with her darling Li. The child is highly amused by this, when the thunderbolt strike isn't aimed at her.

As for the mother, whom the child watches out of the corner of her eye, most of the time she sits in silence; she doesn't seem especially happy. As if she's trying to behave herself, too. As if she's working quite hard at it. Perhaps she's having trouble adapting to the new regulations. Then why does she look at her husband so tenderly? Why the blind acceptance of all his orders? The constant efforts to please him? She even tries to cook, but it always goes wrong. Before, it was the grand-mother who cooked. The mother doesn't know how to do anything, has never taken an interest in household matters. Why, then?

The child knows her mother well enough to realize she's sad. Her eyes, her smile, the few words she utters, her silences, they're sad. The child can tell. But it doesn't have any effect on her. She's only watching. She even thinks she had it coming, her mother did, if she's a little unhappy now.

One evening when the child came racing into the kitchen, she caught her sitting on a stool in tears, and the child immediately ran off: as if, on top of everything else, she would ever console her, the liar. And she went and sat in silence in the dining room, not far from the father, who was casually reading his newspaper.

Something's going on here, something the child can tell is unusual but that she doesn't understand. She thinks about all this, turns it over in her mind, serious, excluded from the adults' conversation, her head full of images, memories, questions, amid the boredom of a never-ending Sunday lunch.

During the day, because no one now looks after her and she's not allowed to make any noise, the child has come up with a game. She takes a tattered doll that she rejected in the old days – she didn't like dolls in the old days – and sits under the dining-room table, which is still covered with the long tablecloth used at mealtimes: she'll be left in peace there, she can't be seen. So she stays there, talking quietly to the tattered doll, commenting on her grievances, going over her resentments. She thinks about everything new in her mother's behaviour, everything new about her disenchantment. And then the child mulls over things she keeps to herself: memories, old problems, unresolved questions. In her head she tries to establish the boundary between dreams and reality, and explores, yet again, the dishonesty displayed by adults.

Like what happened one morning recently.

The child always wakes early, long before her parents. She got up that morning and, bored but afraid of making a noise, she thought she would look out of the dining-room window to see what was going on in the street. She immediately noticed something through the window, something blue and glittery hanging on the railing: a sort of necklace of blue beads, or rather some beads threaded onto a piece of cord, hanging there, with no clue as to how they got there, out of her reach and wafting slightly in the breeze. Such a beautiful sight for the child, such a surprising gift out of nowhere. Without even thinking, she ran to get her mother, who was still in bed, who had to be begged to come and look, and when the mother finally let herself be led, dragged over to the window, the necklace had disappeared. Nothing. There wasn't anything there, not on the balcony, not even in the street below. Nothing to be seen. 'You were dreaming, my darling,' her mother said. Those words again.

Fury from the child. She can still picture the blue sparkle, the fluid swaying of that string of magic beads. You were dreaming. No, I wasn't dreaming, I saw it. Yes, you were dreaming. No, Mummy, I wasn't!

Whatever's happened to the child? She's starting to shout now, and soon she's shrieking, stamping her feet, struggling frantically to get away from her mother, who's trying to calm her. It's not so much because of the necklace, but because she isn't believed. Because she's being lied to. Because her mother's lying to her. That's what it is, that's exactly what it is, like that other time, that time long ago. The child remembers: it's just like with the baby. The baby in Normandy. In a flash the whole thing comes back to her. But she doesn't mention it.

'Liar,' she roars simply. 'Liar!'

'What's going on now?' asks the father from the bedroom, his lie-in interrupted.

'Nothing,' the mother calls, 'nothing, the child just had a dream…'

And she shakes the child by the arm, holding it tightly, as she never has before, ordering her not to say anything, not to say anything. Whatever you do, don't say anything. As if this business with the necklace made her really angry, was so important. And then, without another word, she went back to join her husband.

The child stayed there, choked with sobs and anger. Her mother had hurt her. Why?

Definitely a liar. Like the grandmother. Just another thing she needed to forget.

With the tattered doll's silent support, the child hardened her heart.

They say the Americans are coming. They're going to drive the Germans out. The war will be over.

High time too, says the grandmother, there's nothing left to eat. The big bag of lentils she's been storing at her house is almost empty. Luckily she still has the three hens she keeps in her yard on the rue Bezout and whose eggs she brings over.

The father listens to the radio from morning till night, and sometimes to the station the child doesn't understand at all, the one which is in English one minute and in French the next, but with funny sentences about things like a grandfather's rabbit, lost carrots and other oddities, the station you're not allowed to listen to, apparently.

There's a lot of irritation in the house, and not only on the subject of the Americans. The family's not working properly, the grandmother's wrong to be so pleased, the grandmother doesn't see everything. The child does, though, she's always sniffing out what's going on. The child knows nearly everything.

The child's father and mother argue often, and not always about her. It turns out the mother doesn't behave exactly as she should either. Not exactly as the father would like.

The child watches, listens. And what she sees is strange. Peculiar scenes. The parents are kissing, for example, and then the father's voice starts complaining, quietly at first, but then more loudly. Growing angry. Then the mother cries. She goes out. To run some errands. Visit the grandmother on the rue Bezout.

There were angry words this afternoon, in fact. And with that, the mother headed off. She won't be back till this evening.

The father stays at home, smoking his pipe as he listens to the radio.

As for the child, who's made scenes of her own this afternoon, she's being punished. Her father has just put her out on the landing. For what new misdemeanour, she doesn't know, has already forgotten. But she's not crying. She's grown accustomed to these episodes on the landing, to the clatter of the slammed door and the long wait in the blue shadows of the stairwell. All the same, she nurses her grievances, her rebellion, the shame of being seen in this pitiful situation, alone outside a closed door. At first some neighbours come past, ask what she's doing there, laugh when she says it's a punishment, walk on. Then nothing. Silence. The blue light. Despite her father's instructions to the contrary, she eventually sits down on the stairs. She waits. She thinks this has been going on for a very long time. Perhaps her father will never open the door. Perhaps she's not wanted any more. Well, good.

She almost wants someone to come past, to talk to her. But there isn't a sound. You'd think there's no one left in the building.

But then, as if her wishes have been granted, a door opens at the end of the corridor: where the neighbours they call the Armenians live, a man and a woman who have a sewing workshop in their apartment. The mother doesn't really like them. She says they're on the Germans' side. So she doesn't talk to them: good morning, good evening, that's all. What does 'Armenian' mean? the child wonders.

There, through that half-open door, the child can see two motionless figures. They seem to be hesitating. Then a woman comes towards her, smiling. She's smoking, holding a cigarette in her hand. In a slightly husky voice with a funny accent, she gently tells the child she can come in if she'd like to, that she mustn't stay all alone like this, on the stairs. She doesn't ask the child why she's there. Takes her by the hand.

The child's always been told not to talk to strangers. She also knows she was supposed to stay standing outside her own front door. Her father's order. But that doesn't matter now. Her parents don't matter now. She follows the dark-haired woman with the strange voice. The husband greets them on the doorstep with a silent laugh, shows the child in. What a surprise the place is, comforting, peaceful. The child notices that the man and woman are wearing identical grey overalls, they smile together, look at her in the same calm, attentive way. New, unusual smells around her, of the cigarettes the woman smokes, but also the slightly acrid smell of new fabric, piled up on the roll, of half-finished suits dotted about the place, of sewing-machine oil, and, mingling with all of this, coming from the back of the apartment, there are strong smells of cooking, unfamiliar to the child.

They sit the child down in the workshop. They bring her some peculiar biscuits, some milk and honey. They're kind to her. Very kind. You must come back, says the woman. They don't have children. The child laughs. She feels comfortable. She wonders whether she would rather stay here for ever. She's sleepy.

Perhaps she slept. Looking back, she won't remember. The memory stops with that fantasy about adoption. The bittersweetness of, as she sees it, having left her parents. A feeling of endless time. Of breaking away. A sort of journey.

It's late when she gets home. It's already evening. Evening noises in the building. The light somehow softened, soothed. The Armenian tailor takes the child back to her door. He rings the bell for her. The child's slightly anxious. But the father, who opens the door to them, looking amazed, smiles, not angry at all. Why does he look so happy?

'Oh, the child!' he says. 'Good God! I'd completely forgotten about her... What's the time, then? I'm sorry... Thank you so much... She didn't come knocking on your door, did she?'

And before the Armenian has even finished explaining, the father's talking again.

'It's happened, you know,' he says. 'The Americans have arrived... The first operations were a success...'

'Oh,' the Armenian says simply. 'I see... I'll go and tell my wife.'

They shake hands. The father even invites the Armenian in for a drink, but he declines: he still has work to do. Another time, he says. Another time. And withdraws.

The door closes, leaving the father and child together. They're alone. The mother's still not home.

The father doesn't scold the child this evening. He doesn't criticize her once. He looks at her with a hint of amusement and tenderness in his eye. The child feels that, for the first time since he came home from Germany, he's actually seeing her. He's interested in her.

And then that astonishing thing, with her there, sitting on the sofa beside him, and him sort of dreaming, lost in thought, the sudden gesture.

'What pretty hair you have,' he says. And, just for a moment, she feels the big hand with the freckles smoothing over her hair in a sort of caress.

Was it that evening, the evening of the landings, which would always be the evening of the Armenians in the child's mind, or was it a bit later – because surely things didn't happen that quickly? Anyway, it was at this point in their story that her father took her, awkwardly, onto his lap, just like that, to tell her something. For the first time. Like a normal father. A real father. Like the ones who tell their children stories, in the evening, affectionately, just like that.

It's a funny old story that the father tells the child, a story about trees and farm workers, about carts, grey skies and snow, a story she didn't understand at all – a story from Germany, he said. Most likely she was too surprised, too affected by the novelty of what was happening, to pay attention. So odd sitting on those big enemy knees, being close up to the smell of tobacco, mingled with a subtle fragrance of eau de cologne. And she watches that hand she so dreads, the hand that slaps, and she feels it stroking her hair. It is very gentle now, very soft and attentive.

But oddest of all is hearing this other voice her father has, a voice that isn't scolding, or shouting or being sarcastic. A voice telling a story. A voice talking. A voice talking to her. It's the voice she's listening to. Not the words.

It didn't last very long. Li came home. She went into the kitchen with some provisions and called to her husband. He gently lifted the child onto the floor and got up to go into the kitchen.

Maybe he'd also had enough of having her there, on his lap, the child, all stiff and silent. Maybe she was in his way.

She stayed there, a little dazed, caught up in the surprise of what had happened.

From the grey room with its fading daylight, she could see the light shining from the kitchen, where her mother and father were. But she stayed there, in the darkness, thinking.

One morning, waking in the grey room where they now eat their meals and where the child still has her bed, the child saw that her father was already awake, sitting in the window, apparently writing in the sunlight.

She went over rather fearfully, without making a sound, and he didn't shoo her away. So she stayed there, standing beside him, watching what he was doing in rapt silence.

He was actually drawing, in pencil. And what he was drawing, what the child saw evolving on the page, was a forest of very tall, dense trees planted close together, growing thickly around a clearing. At the far end of the clearing she could make out a long, low house made of logs.

The child didn't move, kept watching.

Then her father took a box of watercolours from his bag and put it on the table. He went to the kitchen to fetch a glass of water – the child didn't move, stayed there, waiting – and put it down next to the box and the drawing, and, apparently unaware of the child, started painting. But she knew he knew she was there. His silence constituted acquiescence. Better: approval. The only sound was the gentle flop-flop of the brush dipped into the water from time to time, and the complicity of the child's breathing, standing there with her hands in the small of her back, behind her father, occasionally catching her breath, attentive to the developing colours on the trees, the sky, the house and the grass on the ground.

When the watercolour was finished, the father sat back slightly so the child could see better.

'Do you like it?' he asked.

The child simply nodded: she did. Then he tore another sheet of white paper from the pad and sat the child down where he'd been sitting. Gave her a pencil.

'Now it's your turn. Draw whatever you like.'

Terrified of her power (and to think she'd always been so bold), she draws a shapeless outline on the paper. To her it's a tree. She says so, very quietly.

And now her father's the one standing behind her, but so tall he has to lean over the child to take her right hand in his and alter – only slightly – the contours of her tree. She lets him guide her, doesn't even think of protesting, because the warmth of that great hand around hers is so wonderful (but oh, how she shrieked if her mother ever took it upon herself to correct her drawings). Then, still holding the little hand, he makes her pick up the brush, makes her load it with water, takes her left hand and guides it with his to show her how to squeeze off the excess water with two fingers, then he swirls the brush round a small pot of green paint and, with both their hands, puts a touch of green on the leaves of their tree.

Swooning with tenderness, the child surrenders to the instructions given by his big hands.

'You see, it's not that difficult!' her father says eventually, flourishing their joint work: a feather duster of green, which the child finds magnificent.

She takes it to her room. Stows it with her precious things.

Where's her mother? She's still asleep. Didn't see. Doesn't know.

That afternoon the father goes out alone. Comes back with a small parcel in his hand. Calls the child.

'Here, this is for you,' he says simply.

The child tears clumsily at the wrapping, in a delicious state of anticipation.

Inside is a tiny box of watercolours: six round blocks of colour and a brush.

'Now,' the father tells her, 'you can work next to me in the mornings.'

The child notices that her mother, who's sitting nearby, has looked up and is watching the scene in silence, unsmiling.

So the child looks away, discreetly.

A strange incident which really surprised the child.

It's Sunday, her grandmother's there. The two women are cooking lunch in the kitchen. The radio is on. A journalist is talking once again about the Normandy landings.

The father comes in to listen. The child follows him. She listens too, to be like the others. And the word suddenly strikes her for the first time. One word. That word.

'In Normandy?' she asks. 'Where we went, me and Mummy and Granny?'

A silence. An extraordinary silence.

The grandmother is first to react.

'In Normandy! As if you've ever been to Normandy!'

The child is about to answer back, to press the point. But she notices her mother, very pale, watching her in the most extraordinary way, as if she's talking to her with her eyes, as if she's screaming at her to be quiet, to stop right there.

'Normandy!' her grandmother says again. 'I ask you! Nonsense! The child talks complete nonsense!'

And the mother adds in a blank voice, 'Maybe she's getting confused with when we went to Ermenonville?'

The conversation trails off. The father hasn't even looked up. He's listening to the radio.

He just gestures to the child to be quiet. A very gentle gesture, very kind, drawing her close to him with his big hand.

How things are changing now, and how quickly it's happening.

The father has an errand to run in town today. As he heads out he announces that, because it's a nice day today, he might as well take the child with him. The mother is a little surprised, but says nothing.

The child is hastily put into her pretty dress, the one from that first day, from the hospital, and she leaves with her father. Alone with her father. It's the first time. The image of her mother, on the doorstep, watching them go.

Out on the street he doesn't tell the child to walk ahead of him: he takes her hand.

The child doesn't talk, intimidated. He doesn't talk either. But the child, who's watching him, can tell he isn't angry, in fact he looks almost cheerful, an expression she's never seen on his face before.

They take the Métro, the father and the child, the father and his daughter, whose hand he holds in the crowds. There are a lot of people in their carriage, but the father finds two seats, sits the child opposite him as if she were a grown-up. The child doesn't know what to make of it. The father takes an old Métro ticket from his pocket.

'Look,' he says.

He folds the ticket lengthways, tears away a bit from near the top-left-hand corner, a bit from near both bottom corners. Then, with a pen, he draws an eye here, some whiskers there, and suddenly the ticket's turned into a dog, one of those funny little short-legged dogs that look like sausages.

'It's a sausage dog,' says the father. '*Dackel* in German. There was one on the farm where I worked.'

The child listens. Doesn't dare ask any questions. Not yet.

'Make another one,' she asks simply.

The father does. The child laughs.

She will hold those two paper dogs carefully in her hand for the whole outing. And once they're back at home, she'll stow them with her precious things, her personal treasures, strange pictures, old toys.

Later, as an adult, she'll never see a dachshund without recalling this scene. And she'll never forget that German name either. *Dackel*.

Is it because it's summer? Is it because everyone's saying the war really is going to end and the Germans are going to be driven out of Paris? There's something in the air, in the streets, and even sometimes in their apartment, despite the arguments between her father and her mother, a kind of lightness; the child can feel it, she experiences it as a huge relief, a sort of happiness that doesn't yet have a name. The father still frequently gets angry but, interestingly, it's not actually so much with the child now as with his wife. With her, the child, the father's hardly ever angry any more. At least, he doesn't shout any more. It's as if he's found a new voice with her. A voice just for her. The child can tell. She's proud of it.

How long is it since the child hugged her mother? Not only has she stopped reaching to put her arms around her neck and cover her with kisses, as she used to, but when her mother tries to catch her on the hop, grab her when she's running past, the child ducks away, races off laughing, doesn't want to be touched any more.

'What's come over you, my darling?' the mother asks, bewildered.

'My name's France,' the child yelps, running to sit at the table.

The father, having heard the exchange, laughs out loud.

'Look, she's more sensible than you are,' he tells his wife.

The child's delighted.

Now when the three of them go out, the child and her parents, it's the father's hand that the child wants to take. It's his hand that she holds, not letting go once for the whole walk. He accepts this. It even seems to make him proud.

One time, he showed Li the child's tiny hand in his, lifting it slightly and opening its delicate fingers in his own palm, and he said, 'Have you seen what pretty hands my daughter has?'

In the evenings it's next to her father, sitting on the sofa in that grey room, that the child comes and nestles gently, in silence, like a small pet, a tamed animal, one that's found its master. While this is going on, Li clears the table, does the washing-up. They're alone, the father and his child. He reads his paper. She stays next to him, not moving or speaking. She's thinking. She's mulling over her ideas, her stories. She'd like to talk to him about them, but she can't yet. She doesn't yet know. Later. She'll do it later, she's sure of that.

In the hush, there's the rustle of the newspaper as the father turns the pages and, from the kitchen, the more distant sound of her mother putting things away. The child lets her mind wander. She looks at the big blotched hand holding the newspaper and now finds it beautiful. It looks a bit like a giraffe's skin, she thinks. The child loves giraffes. In her mind she baptizes her father's hands giraffe-hands. But she doesn't dare tell him. That's silly, he would say.

Sometimes they talk too. He folds up his newspaper. She asks her father to tell her a story. He makes one up. Or he talks about things in Germany. Not sad things. Not about what he went through. Never about what he went through any more. But about what he liked. The forest. The birds. The sounds in the evening. The wind at night. The child listens and listens, full of admiration. She'd like to tell him things too. She has so much to say.

The child feels a helpless trust.

One evening, without thinking, quite spontaneously, she calls her father Daddy for the first time.

All these things inside her head, things she thinks are so clever, the ideas and memories and stories she's been mulling over such a long time, she'd dearly like to share them. She'd like to give them to her father.

She's now just waiting for the moment. She knows it will come. That she'll launch into it.

She looks at her father. She looks at him when they cross the street together. She looks at him when she sits next to him on the sofa. She looks at him when they're sitting up at the table.

She knows for sure she'll talk to him.

It's such glorious weather. Everything seems to have become so easy.

It's at this point that something happens, something that breaks the child's heart: her father has to go back to work. He's so much better now that the doctor pronounces him in good health, physically and mentally, fit for work. He's gone back to his job at the insurance company, his job from before the war. When life was normal. Why? the child asks him. Because I have to. Where do you think money comes from? It makes the father laugh, how naïve the child is.

She still has no concept of money, of material problems. She doesn't understand his going away, leaving her like that, not now that he's her father, his going off all day without her. He seems to be happy, though, he seems glad to be going back to work.

The child is rediscovering the world of before her father. Rediscovering her home as it used to be. But it's as if everything has changed. Disorientated and bored, she wanders around the apartment, which is suddenly empty, pointless, drifting between the mother she's no longer interested in, the mother who actually seems list-less, indifferent, and the grandmother, who's now back with a vengeance, who comes to keep her daughter company during the day, while her son-in-law's away. Her grandmother, who's always busy, feeling important.

Everything's going back to how it used to be and yet nothing's the same.

The conversations between the two women have started again, the whispering and silent nodding. But this complicity, which the child used to loathe, now means nothing to her, barely ruffles her. She thinks about her father. She feels his absence. The grandmother's presence only bothers the child in the sense that she seems to be replacing the father. To have driven him out.

So the child displays her impatience by pulling faces at the old lady, who threatens her exasperatedly: 'You'll see, I'll tell your father.'

The child doesn't worry about this. She's no longer afraid of her father. Because he's her father.

In fact one time, confronted with both women criticizing her, complaining because she's started singing her old warlike songs again, she's suddenly inspired to snap, 'And, anyway, you're liars.'

She doesn't really know what makes her say it. Habit. Or perhaps some sort of instinct.

The mother and grandmother stop talking. Look at each other.

The child, who's now singing again, won't say any more on the subject. She's already vanished under the dining-room table. Her refuge.

The child waits for her father. She waits for him the way you can wait as a child, a way you also can later, in love. She knows it will be a long time, but she waits. She knows he'll be back when evening comes. So she listens out for the sound of the lift, the familiar footsteps on the landing, the rattle of the key in the lock.

And the moment he comes in, even though she knows it annoys her mother, and perhaps him too sometimes – but it doesn't, she can tell it doesn't, isn't she his child now? – she rushes over to him, won't stop until she has his full attention, has secured his affection, taken possession of his big hands.

But the best bit is when, after the grandmother has left and the mother's busy in the kitchen, she finally has her father all to herself.

There. She's sitting next to him, snuggled up to him on the big sofa. She doesn't even want him to read the paper. But the news is very exciting at the moment: they're expecting the Allies to arrive any minute and

Paris to be liberated. The father tries to explain it all to the child. But she doesn't want this. *She* wants to do the talking. She's waited too long. She now wants to say things, all sorts of things.

He laughs, her father does, not understanding what's got into the child, whatever's come over her. He thinks it's funny and sweet.

It will be an evening like this when she speaks.

What makes the child speak isn't her jealousy, her on-going resentment towards her mother. It's not that sort of feeling, she's not old enough for that. It's just the overflowing love she feels for her father, the excessive tenderness and trust, which urges her to give up her most secret thing. To hand it over.

And her admiration for him. The notion that he knows so much. And that *he* speaks the truth. So she's going to ask him the questions no one's ever answered. Those old questions. The ones from the borderline between dreams and reality. That mystery. He must know, surely. He won't be evasive, won't lie like her mother and grandmother.

'You know, Daddy...'

Perhaps that's how she started. In snatches at first, tentative steps, disconnected snippets. The child isn't very artful. Then it all came out. The old story. That memorable trip. Normandy. The hospital. The nurse. The baby. All of it.

In all likelihood a slow, muddled description, punctuated by her father's questions, indulgent at first, amused and then increasingly urgent, incisive, irritated, brutal.

Then there's a blank, emptiness. Something happened, something the child didn't understand, a sort of cataclysm which turned everything upside down, abruptly turned her father into someone completely different, made him go very pale and say in an altered voice that she's *talking nonsense* – the very expression the women had used – and made him tell her to shut up, made him shove her aside and get to his feet, and, in a flash, shattered the harmony of that evening.

From that moment on, everything's confused for the child. She'll remember only that she was left on her own, looking mechanically through the pictures in a book that was lying around, so upset she couldn't see anything, while her parents shut themselves away in the kitchen, and from there came the disturbing sounds of an argument, muted at first and then growing more and more violent, an argument in which she could pick out the interwoven patterns of their two voices, her mother's whispering and tearful, and her father's harsh and angry.

No one puts the child to bed that evening. She ends up falling asleep on the sofa, filled with the sadness of having failed to secure an answer to her question and with an obscure, very distant sense of having said the wrong thing.

When the child wakes the next morning, very early, in the bed she must have been carried to while she was asleep, she can tell something's happened. There's an unusual silence in the apartment. Has her father already left this morning? Isn't he having breakfast with them? Everything looks different today... The mother, who's telling the child to get up, has an upside-down face. The face she has on tearful days. She's obviously been crying a lot. She hasn't done her hair, hasn't put on her make-up. She's wearing an old dress, a boring, ugly one. She sits next to the child, on the bed, and explains in a funny-sounding voice, an odd voice, that she won't be able to look after her for a few days, that she's going to take her to her grandmother.

Consternation. The child protests. Why? When? What about the Americans coming to Paris? And other armies too, her father told her, he promised he'd take her to see... he explained it all to her... She wants to see the soldiers, the tanks, everything... It must be soon, her father said...

Her mother says that that's just it, it'll be dangerous, that the grandmother's neighbourhood is quieter. The father will come to fetch the child when it's all over, when Paris has been liberated. When the Germans have left.

The child cries. The mother won't budge. Counters her tears with icy silence. She gets the child ready, the child crying, protesting. The mother's face is unreadable, like a stranger's. Her movements are hard, abrupt, like an enemy's.

She packs the child's bag, and the child watches these preparations fearfully. She's never been away from her mother. She's never been anywhere alone. She doesn't understand what's going on at all. Why isn't her father here?

She tries to throw herself into her mother's arms, to kiss her; she begs her. The mother pushes her away gently but firmly. Just because, she says. That's the way it is. Be sensible. You'll come back. It's not for long. Your daddy will come to fetch you.

The mother's talking in short, resolute sentences which tear the child apart. She's never talked to her like this. Perhaps it's this shift, this difference, this strangeness, this *strangerness*, that hurts the child. Her mother's no longer her mother, but someone she doesn't know.

They take the Métro, the two of them. Like on that first day, that day long ago when they went to see the father. The mother holds the child's hand, but anyone would think she doesn't love her, that she's angry; she doesn't talk, and there's a harshness about her fingers that the child doesn't recognize, that almost hurts her.

The child has stopped protesting, deep in the despair of her exile but of something else too, something more serious that she doesn't understand. She can't begin to grasp it, but it's there. Between them. In that silence.

Of her time with her grandmother, the time in August 1944 – how long was it? A few days, a week, more? – the child would remember almost nothing. Apart from waiting. She waited, waited day after day for it to be over. For someone to come for her. For her father to come for her. She thought he would be the one to come.

She keeps asking the grandmother when she can go home. Aren't you happy with me, then? is the grandmother's only reply. She tries to teach the child to sew. She shows her how to throw grain for the three hens she keeps in the yard behind her house. She introduces her to the few customers who are starting to come back. During fittings, the women chatter, look at the child, try to get her to talk.

The child's bored. Filled with despair.

Just one image from that time, the wallpaper featuring bunches of roses in the bedroom where she sleeps alone. It's cold in this room, even in August, because the shutters are always closed. Some idea of the grandmother's. The child's afraid to turn the light out. So she stays there for a long time, gazing at the roses on the walls, before she goes to sleep.

One evening she's already been in bed quite a while when she thinks she hears talking downstairs: she thinks she recognizes her father's voice, down there, along with the grandmother's. They're talking loudly. Shouting even. Half asleep, the child gets straight out of bed, goes downstairs in the dark… But she must have made a noise: the grandmother looms in front of her, orders her back to bed this minute. But, the child says. No buts. You were dreaming. There's no one here.

And the next morning, nothing. The usual waiting.

And then one morning there's such a noise outside, shots fired, shouting, a great thundering of lorries making the house shake, more shouting, firecrackers, cheers…

'Thank the Lord!' cries the grandmother, who's been at the windows since dawn. 'Here they are! They're coming! It's them! It's the liberation! We're saved!' And she runs all over the house to get a better view, from the best window, calls to her neighbours, more excited than the child's ever seen her. The child thinks her grandmother's being unbearable.

'What about me, when am I going home?' asks the child.

'Later,' says the grandmother. 'Your parents have had their talk anyway.'

'About what?'

'About things that are none of your business,' says the grandmother.

The father had promised he'd take the child to see the soldiers on the day of the liberation. The liberation's here now. He wasn't telling the truth. The grandmother's liberation, this particular liberation here, is of little interest to the child. And anyway, you can hardly see anything from her windows. The child is filled with sadness.

There is one extraordinary thing, though, one moment: that incredible huge peal of bells which seemed to come from all the churches at once. The grandmother had opened the windows, all the windows and all the shutters, windows and shutters opened at last to the summer and those tumultuous bells, and the old woman cried and pulled a funny face. It's over, she said, the war's over. We're free. And she took the child in her arms, she kissed her. Which really surprised the child: her grandmother never cried, never kissed her. Mind you, her hands were still just as cold.

And she was the one who, the next day, or a bit later, it's no longer clear, told the child she would take her back to her parents. The father probably hadn't been able to come. Or perhaps he'd forgotten.

The day the child comes back is a Sunday. Everyone will be at home, she thinks; we'll all have lunch together. It'll be just like before. The child drags her grandmother by the hand to get there more quickly and talks nineteen to the dozen. My word, will you ever stop! says the grandmother, but she's not really angry. The child laughs. In fact everyone looks happy, out in the street, in the Métro. You can tell the Krauts have left, the old woman says. And it's about time we had something to be happy about. She sighs, the grandmother does, talking to herself, muttering between her teeth about things the child doesn't understand, doesn't listen to. The child is entirely absorbed in her delight at being back in the city, and she can't stop looking around, listening, seeing how pretty everything looks: there seem to be parties going on everywhere, with flags in all directions, people laughing, music on every street corner, lots of people on café terraces. The child keeps thinking they'll be there soon, she'll see her parents again. She can't believe her luck.

On the way her grandmother gives the child advice that she more or less hears: she must be a good girl, she must leave her parents alone, not talk nonsense – you know very well what I mean. Her father's tired, and her mother too, she mustn't pester them, etc. All through the partying streets, the old woman's nagging voice doesn't really reach the child's ears as her heart thumps impatiently at the thought of going home.

But when they get there, when the grandmother rings the bell the first time, no one comes to the door. They listen. Everything's quiet. Perhaps they've gone out, says the grandmother. She rings again. More waiting. The child's frightened, she's not really sure why, but she's frightened. At last they hear footsteps. And it's her father who opens the door. The father looking all strange, or rather similar to how he'd been when the child first met him, even more upright, by the looks of him, more severe, more distant.

He says hello to the grandmother, but takes the child in his arms, without a word. He carries her to the dining room, strokes her hair, looks at her, looks at her as if he's discovering her.

The child barely has time to believe it's happening before he puts her down, takes his jacket from the back of a chair and goes out, leaves, closing the door behind him.

'I'll be off, I'll be off,' the grandmother says quickly. 'I'll just say hello to Li, I'm not having lunch with you…'

The father's already left, without responding to her words. But where's the mother?

The grandmother calls in vain. The child finds no one in the kitchen. The grandmother opens the bedroom door: Li is lying down, asleep. Curtains drawn. On the bedside table there are pills.

'Is she ill?' asks the child, who's come over and is gazing in awe at her mother's face, unreadable in sleep, at her pallor, her mess of hair.

The grandmother wakes her daughter and she opens her eyes at last. She looks so peculiar, so befuddled, that the child instinctively backs away. She doesn't want her mother to touch her. To kiss her.

But no. Nothing like that happens. The mother just says – but in a strange, thick, lazy voice – it would be better if the grandmother left, that it'll be OK now.

'Are you sure?' the old lady asks.

'Absolutely. What's the time? Anyway, the child can help me…'

She gets out of bed, puts on a dressing gown and sees the grandmother to the door. The old lady very swiftly slips away.

The child and her mother are left alone. The child frozen in a sort of dread that her mother might want to kiss her. But nothing happens.

The mother, still in her dressing gown, an old pink dressing gown that the child doesn't like, drifts about the place, puts a few things away. The child notices that the apartment's very untidy, with clothes on the furniture, the kitchen in a mess, full of dirty dishes.

'We're going to have lunch,' says the mother. 'I'm bound to find something.'

Outside in the street they can hear a band playing. A woman singing. People join in the chorus.

The child goes off to play under the dining-room table, reunited with her old doll.

Her suitcase, which the grandmother left in the hall by the door, is still there; but perhaps her father will put it away when he comes home.

Of the weeks, the few months that come next, what will one day be left in the child's memory? A few images, a few snatches of meaning taken from an obscure, muddled, mysterious continuum?

Since she came home everything's been so strange, her parents' behaviour so peculiar. The child doesn't understand any of it. Not lovey-dovey any more, the parents aren't. Don't talk to each other now, or look at each other, and suddenly start arguing. About everything and nothing: Li's untidiness, her lethargy, which 'goes with all the rest of it', her inability to run a household, and then there's the way she dresses, the money she spends. The same old criticisms, but more needling now, spiteful. The father shouts. The mother cries. And then she shouts too. Sometimes they go and shut themselves in the bedroom or the kitchen to shout louder. The child can't hear the words then, but she understands the tone of voice.

Sometimes the grandmother comes over and it's worse; the three of them shut themselves in the kitchen and then they talk so loudly, the grandmother's voice is so squeaky, the father's so violent, that the child only clutches at words in passing, strange words: *Too young. Your fault. Indulgent. Lies. Shameful. Why? Disgusting.* Then she hears her mother crying, uncontrollably, like a child.

The child can't believe it. Grown-ups and their mad goings-on. But she continues playing under the table. She's perfectly all right under the table, with her old doll. She brushes the doll's hair for ages and ages, waiting for it to be over, this performance in the kitchen, waiting for the door to open and for them to come out, with the funny faces they have then. After these arguments the grandmother usually picks up her coat in a dignified way and leaves.

And when the father isn't there, when he's gone to work, when she's left alone with her mother, that's a whole other story, and the child can't be sure she prefers it. Then there's a very special kind of silence in the apartment. An icy silence. A terrifying silence.

The mother gets up late. Gives the child something to eat, dresses her without a word. Then she drifts from one room to another, irritated to have the child there, hanging around not knowing what to do with herself. Every now and then the mother starts to cry, and the child is frightened by the puffy, deformed red face her tears give her.

She asks her mother to put the radio on. She needs to hear something, some music, songs, the announcers' reassuring voices. It's so cheerful now, the radio: military marches, love songs, jazz, the news delivered in a jaunty voice. The child listens to everything. Indiscriminately.

In fact one day she hears them say on the news that the war really is over, that all the prisoners will be coming home. Families will be able to pick them up at the Gare de l'Est. The child runs to tell her mother. But why does this make her cry and then laugh?

Her mother really has become very strange.

In among all this, it's as if no one sees the child any more. Almost as if she's become invisible. No one has time for her now. She is there, though.

When the father comes home in the evening he hardly even kisses her. An absent-minded stroke of her hair as he comes in, acknowledging that she's been waiting for him, standing in that awkward way she now has. A stroke of his big hand with its freckles. And then, straight away, the arguing starts with the mother, the shouts and tears.

The child would dearly like to be interesting. She follows the conversation as best she can. She watches and listens. She hopes her father will acknowledge her presence, her attentiveness. She comes running at the least sign of conflict, waiting for an opportunity to get involved, to make her father understand that she's there, with him.

One image in all this confusion will become a memory: the business of the accounts book.

The father feels they're spending too much in this household. Can't think where the money's going. Is flabbergasted. Appalled. He's asked Li to keep a record of her daily expenses from now on and has bought her a special book for this. A book the child thinks is glorious. On the glossy hard cover there are birds in every colour and on the inside is a printed page for each day of the week. Some days later he asks to check through it. The mother can't find it. Has she lost it? Mislaid, she says, I've just mislaid it. She'll find it, it's bound to be somewhere.

A silent stare from the father. The sign of an impending storm.

The child, who watches everything and sees everything, darts off without a word: she thinks she might have seen the book under a sideboard, it must have fallen off. It's been lying around there for a few days. And she brings it back triumphantly, hands it to her father, expecting congratulations.

But nothing. The child needn't have bothered.

The father leafs through the accounts book, finds its virgin pages empty of any annotation.

The child sees her father's face alter as he flicks through it. He looks at his wife, looks at the child. Starts shouting.

'Even this child's more sensible than you! We can give this book of yours to her, she'll make better use of it!'

And with these words he hurls the book across the room, where it bounces off a wall. Then he takes his jacket and goes out, slamming the door.

Li bursts into tears.

The child rushes over to pick up the accounts book, which is the worse for wear, its spine broken and its pages crumpled. Never mind. She starts leafing through it with some satisfaction. It feels to her as if she's won it. It belongs to her now, her father said. Armed with a pencil, she starts methodically marking every page with her usual signs.

And yet, couched within her victory is the sadness, the anxiety, at feeling that roughened broken cover with her little fingers.

The child so desperately wants to get the facts straight that an odd idea comes into her head one day. She can see that it's Li the father's angry with, it's because of Li that everything's going wrong. The child convinces herself she needs to show her father just how well she, the child, his child, understands him. If she wants to be in favour with him.

One evening when *they* are arguing, without even taking the precaution of shutting themselves away to do their shouting, the child thinks she sees a way. This time she can show clearly which side she's on.

While they shout and as good as come to blows, the child sneaks into the bedroom. On the dressing table is a boxed set of perfumes – three exquisite bottles – that the father gave to Li shortly after he came home. Prestigious white casing, finely edged with gold lines. The perfumer's name inscribed in black letters. The child traces its magnificent outline with her finger.

Perfectly obvious the mother no longer deserves it.

The child opens the box, respectfully, reverently. Hesitates a moment. Makes up her mind. Takes the stopper from one of the bottles. Inhales swooningly. Empties the contents into the basin. Repeats the procedure with the other two.

The smell must be so penetrating, with the three perfumes unleashed, that the door opens. Li comes in. Screams. The child's father appears, understands immediately.

The child watches him and him alone. Ashen, silent, frozen. At last he comes over to her. Still a moment of doubt, of hesitation? But no, he slaps the child, calmly and hard, to the right, then the left, that way he does. Like before. Like when he didn't love her.

'Put her straight to bed without any supper,' he says coldly to his wife.

The child doesn't shed a single tear. Too stunned. It's her mother who's crying, as usual.

Later, in bed, the child hears the door to the landing slam. Her father's gone out. He'll be back later.

For a long time the apartment would still have the persistent smell of that evening.

Another evening, an evening when the father and mother had had a particularly vehement row, without even really shouting, but with hard, definitive little sentences, with nasty glowering looks that the child knows well, the father went out alone again.

That was when this surprising thing happened: the mother came to look for the child and sat her on her lap for the first time in a very long time. The child didn't move, waiting. And the mother talked to her gently, almost calmly, without crying.

'You know, my darling, your father may leave. Leave for good. He won't stay with us.'

'Oh,' the child said simply.

The mother started kissing her, saying sweet nothings to her, as she used to. The child received her attention passively, her thoughts elsewhere.

Her mother does talk nonsense.

*

And, letting herself down from her mother's lap, the child went off along the corridor singing very loudly, stamping her feet on the floor, the way she'd seen soldiers do.

In this confusion, though, there would still be Christmas, there would still be that day. The first Christmas the child would spend with her father, and it was to be the only one. But that she didn't yet know.

No memories in the child's mind of previous Christmases. Perhaps she was too young. Perhaps also – because of the war, the lack of money, the loneliness and plenty of other factors – the festivities had been more or less skipped.

But this time there is a Christmas.

The child wakes one morning to the surprising smell of the fir tree that's been brought into the grey room while she was sleeping, an acrid yet fresh smell which makes her open her eyes. And she sees this tree which has appeared mysteriously, this piece of woodland which seems to have come from the forests her father's told her about, and, at the foot of the tree, colourful parcels, tied with ribbons. The child is dumbstruck. It's as miraculous an apparition as those blue beads hanging on the balcony.

The father and mother are there, apparently calmer. They're smiling; they look a little sad, thinks the child. Particularly the father. But he's here, and he looks at her as he used to, as he did when she was his little girl and he thought she had such pretty hands.

They tell her all this is for her. She doesn't understand. Everything's incomprehensible this morning, and that's what's wonderful. It's at this point that she notices things in the tree, a multitude of little paper figures hanging from the branches or standing on them. Later she'll know it was her father who drew them, coloured them and cut them out. These are what she wants to touch, to pick up. She's told she must open her presents first. See what's in the boxes. But there are too many things, she doesn't know where to start. Perhaps her feeling of happiness is in all this excess? Right down to the sound of bells which now start pealing, like that strange day, Liberation day, when her grandmother cried. Everything's miraculous, even the sun, which hasn't been seen for days and which suddenly fills the room, unexpected and glorious.

The image the child retains, that sticks in her memory, is of her father now sitting in an armchair and her, the child, standing between his legs. He's the one opening the presents and she watches. But she's more affected by the magic of the moment – the smells, the soft scrunching of paper, the sound of bells ringing, the light, having her father back – than the contents of those boxes and bags.

Christmas isn't presents, it's that moment.

Is it on that morning? Is it another, shortly afterwards, closely associated with Christmas morning in the child's mind? It snowed… Through the window, on the roof-tops, out in the street, everything's white. She's never seen snow before, or at least has never been aware of it.

She goes outside with her father and discovers this tremendous oddity. Wrapped up snugly, holding her father's hand, in all that whiteness which creaks so surprisingly underfoot, she's intoxicated with the chill of it and a sense of freedom. And of tenderness too.

'Don't stay out too long,' said Li, who was preparing a big meal, in her own way.

But for now the child and her father are walking through this miracle of snow. The world belongs to them. Life itself.

Just an impression the child has.

Christmas was for show. A show put on for one day. A pause. Or perhaps a full stop.

There will be no miracle, no miracle at all. Only very natural things. The child doesn't understand what's going on, what's happening now. And yet she is obscurely aware of its threat all around her.

Your father may leave, her mother had said one day. She hasn't said it again. She hasn't talked about it. But the child hasn't forgotten.

Interestingly, there's no more arguing at home now, no more shouting. Something very different has started. The father's become peculiarly distant, and silent. The father and mother no longer talk to each other, they avoid each other. And it's in this silence between them that something mysterious has evolved. Something frightening. Unbearable.

It's so odd when the father comes home in the evenings now. He ignores the mother. Hardly talks to the child.

And on Sundays the father must realize that things aren't right, that it can't go on. He most likely knows all this. So he often takes the child out for a little walk, alone with him. But it's not like before. The child doesn't feel important, as she used to, when she really was his little girl.

And she feels as if she's somehow stealing these moments. Has no right to them. But those aren't her words. She can't put her uncomfortable feeling into words.

One image from those walks will live on in her mind. For a long time.

It's almost spring. The child's wearing a blue coat. She'll remember that blue.

Her father's holding her hand, but he isn't talking. He seems sad, the child thinks, leaning to the side from time to time so she can see his face, check on his mood. She's always worried, the child is, about her father's frame of mind. He, though, doesn't look at her, he doesn't see her. He's walking a little too quickly for her, his eyes unseeing, his head full of goodness knows what. He seems to be somewhere else. But there is still his hand, firmly holding the child's hand, his warm, familiar hand, rough and soft all at the same time, the friendly giraffe-hand.

The father and child walk unsmiling through the indifferent crowd, through that Sunday's shouts, noises and music. The father walking blindly with the child, who feels like a part of him.

And there in a square stands a merry-go-round with wooden horses circling to stilted music, a barrel organ spilling out an old-time tune. The child thinks it's lovely, the horses turning, the strange music. She drags her father gently by the hand to show him, to tear him away from his thoughts.

He thinks she's asking for a ride on the merry-go-round.

'Do you want to have a ride? Is that it?'

The child nods, solemn. It's easier.

The merry-go-round happens to stop then anyway. The father hoists the child astride a horse, secures her properly, carefully, with the strap.

'You're sure you won't fall? Will you hold on?'

The child smiles, happy at his concern, his attention. She's a child who has a father; that's what she thinks in a muddled way, fleetingly, with pride.

The merry-go-round sets off and the plaintive organ music starts up again. The child clutches the vertical pole that runs through her horse, fixing it to the platform and the brightly painted dome.

And every time she passes her father, as the ride turns, she looks at him. There he is, standing among the other parents. But he doesn't seem to see anything, miles away, lost in thought. He's not watching the child.

Then all of a sudden she feels very strongly that he's going to leave, that he's in the process of leaving now and she won't be able to see him again. She wants to get off this horse, to stop everything, to stop this thing which is now happening, which will carry on happening, going on and on, like the merry-go-round.

When the ride finally comes to an end, it's the old man who runs it who unhitches her. She throws herself into her father's arms. He's amazed by this show of emotion. He doesn't understand. He's already gone.

On a few more occasions, when the father gets home – he comes back from the office later and later now – he goes to sit next to the child on the sofa in the dining room, or on the edge of her bed if she's already gone down. He asks her what she's done today, whether she's been good, if everything's all right. That sort of thing. The father isn't very imaginative these days. The child always gives the right answer: everything's always all right, isn't it? He seems satisfied, even though she thinks she can see something like sadness in his eyes. Perhaps it's just boredom: nowadays the father often seems slightly removed from what he's saying, or what he's looking at.

The child asks him, as she used to before, to tell her a story. The one about the forest and the dwarves. He starts. Then he realizes she's not following it, not listening. And he's right, it's not the story she's hearing. It's his voice she's listening to, as she thinks about very difficult things.

Then the father gets annoyed and walks away.

The evening when the father didn't come home for the first time, the child waited an age. She waited for him like a woman in love. Helplessly. She waited after supper. And even long after she'd been put to bed. He didn't come.

He didn't come home the next day either, and she waited again.

She will always remember this new kind of waiting. The furious need to hear his voice, to be reunited with the smell of his pipe, with the freckles on his hands. His giraffe-hands. To touch them. To play with them. And to talk to him. To say what? She doesn't know. But she would know, she thinks, if he were there. She'd know.

She waits, huddled in a corner by the door. She listens out for the familiar sound of the lift, footsteps on the landing. It's never him. He's still not back. She waits.

The child's mother walks past, sees her, and tells her not to hang around there like that, he won't come back. In fact he'll never come back. My darling. He's left them.

The child doesn't say anything. She doesn't understand these words. She doesn't believe what she's being told. Anything her mother tells her. She escapes the clutches of this woman who wants to touch her, to talk to her, her mother with her tears and her ugly face, she ducks away from her brutally, she doesn't want to see her, or hear her. She runs away to the grey room where her bed is, and there, next to her bed, she sits on the floor and shunts her toys around on the carpet, singing to herself.

The grandmother, who just so happens to be there, strays from room to room, muttering goodness knows what.

Over her words, the neighbours' radio keeps up its noise. It's suppertime, as if everything's normal.

Peculiar days now for the child. With her father's absence, everything seems to have become absence. Hazy images, muted sounds, indistinct words, lost in indifference.

It's a world of absence. The child has become absence too.

She is living, though. And one thing proves she's even reverted to being as difficult and capricious as she was before her father came home: she's gone back to smothering the walls with drawings and signs in coloured crayon, with complete impunity. It doesn't seem to bother anyone any more.

'Your father lives in a different house now,' the mother says one day.

Just like that. Incidentally. She's holding a letter in her hand.

And this, for once, the child takes in. Is it the word *house* that strikes her, that creates an image? In any event, it's enough. She takes it in. She learns this fact, this news, that her father has left. This time her mother's telling the truth.

The mother hasn't cried for a while now. Her face is blank, severe, altered. She dresses badly. In clothes she used to wear for doing housework. She doesn't wear make-up. She looks like an old woman. She looks more and more like the grandmother.

They're facing each other, the child and her mother, both serious, and the child feels like a grown-up looking across at another grown-up.

The mother doesn't try to kiss her, to draw her close. No. She looks at her seriously. And the child understands this look.

The child doesn't ask any questions. Her mother goes on to tell her that her father wants her to know he'll come to see her. Soon.

When's soon? thinks the child. But she doesn't ask anything, doesn't say anything. She's just anxious at the thought of this visit she'd stopped hoping for – well, almost stopped – this visit with its terribly sketchy outline, this visit she can't picture.

When? What will *he* say? What will *he* do? And then what when the visit's over? Will he really leave? How will he go about it? And what about her, the child, what will she say? What should she do?

Days go by.

The evening her father appears, the child has no warning. The mother probably has none either. The bell rings. The mother calls to the child to open the door, which is a struggle for her, given her height. And she suddenly finds herself confronted with her father's stature. She'd already forgotten how tall he is. She can't speak. It's too soon for the child. Too difficult. Wrong-footed, she doesn't say a thing, tilts her head to receive the kiss her father leans forward to give her.

He sits in the grey room. Looks around like a traveller returning to a forgotten country. The child follows him. But then Li suddenly appears in the kitchen doorway, theatrical, eyes shining, monopolizing the scene. And words fly, the argument begins, voices are raised here and there. Not for long. The mother's wonderful assurance is snapping already and she's crying, as she stands there by the door, like a broken thing.

Meanwhile the child has come and sat silently on the sofa, beside her father, who's still talking loudly, not looking at her.

Li abandons the fight, slamming the door behind her.

The father turns to the child. He doesn't say anything. He looks at her. How he looks at her. And, what with the tenderness in his eyes, the child looks away.

He also looks at the drawings splattered over the walls. He looks at them slowly, in detail. The child is rather frightened.

'It doesn't matter,' the father says simply.

And this time when he pulls her to him to sit her on his lap, she puts up no resistance.

They stay like that for a while, in silence. He holds her close to him, and she rediscovers the forgotten warmth and the smell of tobacco and eau de cologne which, for her, already belongs to before.

And then he peels himself away from her, gently, gets up and leaves.

The father's visits are now more or less regular. In fact he's been asked, please, from now on, to let them know in advance when he's coming. He arrives on Saturday or Sunday and always brings something for the child, a surprise. A toy. Some sweets. An orange. A scarf.

When he gets there the child first spies out the bag, wrapping paper or envelope with the new object inside it. It's not so much the type of present she's interested in, as what it means to her. More or less affection from her father. His interest in her. She needs to gauge it.

Once her father has left, the new present joins the others, with her treasures, her precious secret treasure trove where so many things are now hoarded together, a wooden Pinocchio, a mechanical chick, two bars of American chocolate, some acid drops, a woolly hat she never wears for fear of losing it, the fateful accounts book, the two sausage-dog-shaped Métro tickets and the box of paints. All hidden under her bed. Luckily, no one does much cleaning in the house. Particularly now.

During the father's visits, Li is always there threatening to intervene, to make a scene or cry. And sometimes even the grandmother, often on Sundays, pulling an extraordinary face and sidling into the room when she's least expected, with her thin old lady's light-footed step.

The father and the child don't talk much, and his visits never last long anyway.

'Next time I'll take you to a restaurant,' the father says one day.

The restaurant day is a Sunday. The mother has dressed the child in her blue coat and her black patent-leather shoes, now rather tight, with white socks pulled up high. Her hair's been well brushed but no one tries curling it any more. It doesn't matter. It'll be fine as it is. The mother's tired. The grandmother, who's there, has her important-days face.

The child waits for her father.

She's ready. She thinks she looks gorgeous and wonders when he'll arrive. She's been going round in circles in the apartment for a long time now, pacing in her little shoes, which make an irritating noise on the wooden floor.

'Calm down,' the grandmother scolds. 'Stay still for a minute, for God's sake! You'll drive us mad!'

The mother's irritable too, shuts herself in the kitchen 'to avoid seeing *him*'.

At the first ring of the doorbell, the child runs to open the door. The father doesn't come in: he kisses the child and, as no one's appeared, he calls out that he'll 'bring *her* back at about five'.

There, they've left, the father and his child. Alone. Hand in hand. Her little hand reunited with her father's big hand.

Her black shoes patter swiftly down the stairs…

But there's already something panicking the child. She's thinking about the question her mother has told her to ask her father, the words she's been made to practise and which she'll have to pronounce: 'Daddy, are you going to come back to us?' Tricky. The child's well aware of that. When to say it? Now or later? And how? It bothers the child terribly, this problem does, as they walk along the street in silence, she and her father. She decides to put it off till they're having lunch.

For now she's trying to think only of this moment, of this hand holding hers at last, of the tall familiar figure beside her, a figure which leans over from time to time and asks if everything's all right, if they're not walking too quickly, if she's happy. Can you hear me, France?

Yes, of course everything's all right; no, they're not walking too quickly, but even so. The child trots along to keep up with her father, gives one-word answers. Happy, yes, very. But the thought of the question she must ask comes back to her. The child falls silent.

They take the Métro. They take the Métro as they did before. As they did that time with the Métro-ticket dogs. But today the father doesn't seem to be thinking about ticket dogs, or anything like that. What's he daydreaming about exactly, with such a serious face? No knowing.

He doesn't say anything. He doesn't see anything either, apparently, his eyes lost, gazing at a spot just above the child who's sitting facing him. She, the child, is looking at him with all her might. Actually, she rather likes it when he's distracted.

Where are they going? It feels like a long way, possibly further than she's ever been in Paris. But, anyway, that's not what she's interested in, not where they're going, the name of the place, whether it's near or far, not that sort of thing. She's with her father, she's going to have lunch with her father, she has her father all to herself for the whole day.

Now they're out in the street again, in an unfamiliar neighbourhood. The child is connected to the known world, to security, only by her father's hand. And she thinks that's nice. He can take her where he likes. He takes care of her. He's her father.

He asks her whether she's hungry. Now there's a question. To please him she says that yes, she's hungry. He looks happy. 'We'll be there soon,' he says, and he looks happier by the minute.

But now the thought of her mission has come back to haunt the child and, once again, she can feel anxiety creeping over her. When? Before lunch? During it? Afterwards maybe?

'Here we are,' says her father.

He opens a glazed door and goes in with the child close behind him. She's never been to a restaurant before, never gone into a place like this. She's dazed by the noise, the bustle, the lights, the smells. Following in her father's wake, the child gamely steps further into this strange world, amid the hubbub of voices, the clink of cutlery and the bright newness of the lighting.

Meanwhile, her father's heading straight for one of the tables, by the window. A small table covered with a white tablecloth like the others. Now, there's a lady sitting at this particular table, a lady who's looking at the child and smiling.

'France,' the father says, 'I'd like to introduce you to a friend: Agnès.'

The child is taken aback. She doesn't understand. He must have got this wrong. She stands next to her father and stares at this stranger, this pretty, young, blonde, nicely made-up, well-dressed, smiling stranger. And everything happens very quickly. The father gets the child to sit down, sits down himself. He takes the chair facing the woman; the child is in the middle, between them. The father says something. What? The child doesn't know. The lady carries on smiling with her pretty lips, smoothed over with dazzling red, and her pretty teeth. She just won't stop smiling, her eyes on the father one moment and the child the next. And the father, well, he just won't stop talking. The child doesn't grasp, doesn't hear what he's saying.

The waiter comes to take their order and the child can't tear her eyes away from this woman with her perpetual smile. But now the lady's talking, the red lips are moving very quickly. Her voice is soft, musical, pleasing – and yet the child can't make out any words. Actually, what was the question her mother told her to ask?

In fact she, the child, is the one who's being asked something. When it comes to questions, it's the lady who's doing the asking, leaning towards her slightly: *Does this big girl go to school yet, then?* Of course not, of course she doesn't go to school, the child mutters inwardly, giving just a shake of her head in reply. *Not bored all on her own?* What a thought. The child shakes her head furiously.

She's so sweet! Shame she's lost her tongue… Or hasn't she? Has she?

The conversation falters. Or rather is reduced to an exchange between the lady and the child's father, over her head, given they're facing each other, as her father and mother used to before, the child now thinks. But here, is it because of the noise, in order to talk and hear each other, these two lean slightly closer together over the table, which is so narrow that it wouldn't take much for their heads to touch. And with them there are no arguments.

Their food arrives. The child has no idea what she's eating. She'll never know. But what she does know is that it's not going down.

'Eat up, then,' says her father, as he used to at home; and it feels very funny to the child, those same words,

words she hasn't heard for a long time. But what's changed is that he's saying them very gently. Not angry at all.

And now the question she's meant to ask comes back to her all of a sudden. What if I asked now? thinks the child. But just then she sees something, something that catches her attention, something extraordinary.

There across the table, her father's hand, the big rust-speckled hand she knows so well, the giraffe-hand, the hand that belongs to her, the child, has just come down over that small, elegant white hand with the red nail varnish which was resting meekly next to the plate: the lady's hand.

Time stands still.

The child won't remember anything of the rest of the meal, nor how it ended. Anything of what was said, what happened, what was eaten or what she herself didn't eat. *Oh, it doesn't matter, leave it, it's all right…* Yes, her father said those words, very sweetly, that much she does remember. You'd think nothing matters any more for the father.

No memories at all, up until the moment when she was alone with him again, walking through the streets, after the lady had left, the lady who'd wanted to kiss her goodbye.

'You'll see her again soon,' the father said as they walked away. 'I love her very much, you know.'

The child said nothing. It's true, she lost her tongue that day.

The father and child walk back through the streets they came along that morning. They're both thinking about all sorts of things. And then the father asks the child what she thought of the lady. The child thinks. She ends up saying she doesn't know.

'But you do think she's pretty, don't you?' the father says, not letting it drop.

Yes, the child thinks she's pretty. She won't say more than that. That will be all for today. She's tired.

The father gently squeezes the child's hand in his. But the child thinks of the lady's white hand, and her own hand stays inert.

When they arrive home, the child's father takes her all the way to the door, kisses her and then leaves, very quickly, as usual.

The child realizes she hasn't asked the wretched question.

When her mother appears and asks how she got on with her task, she says she forgot.

That night the child has a strange dream. She's in the local square with her mother, as she so often used to be. Her mother is sitting on a bench alone and the child's not far away, playing with a ball. It's a beautiful day. The mother's wearing a very pretty dress, a red one, and her nails are painted red too.

All of a sudden someone arrives, someone the child doesn't immediately recognize. But yes, of course, it's her father, wearing the blue jumper he wore to the restaurant and with his pipe in his hand. He sits down next to the mother and talks to her, right up close. They're not at all angry, quite the opposite; he's put an arm around her shoulders, like lovers do, and they're looking at each other the way they used to, when the father came home.

And the child feels something inside her, an odd, a very odd kind of contentment.

But just then she wakes up. The feeling of happiness lasts a little longer. And a little longer. And disappears.

Now the father comes to pick up the child every other Sunday. Sometimes the blonde lady is there, sometimes she isn't.

The last time the child is to be alone with her father he suggests taking her outside in the fresh air, onto the fortifications at the old city gate, the Porte des Lilas. The child thinks this lilac-scented name is pretty, but you know, her father says, there are no lilacs there. Even so, the child says.

It's a Sunday afternoon. Her father didn't come to pick her up till after lunch. He seems in a good mood. In fact he seems in a much better mood since he left home.

It's a lovely day. In the bus they stood on the platform at the back, which delighted the child.

Once there, at the fortifications (the father also calls it *the wastelands*, an expression the child rather likes), there are sorts of hills and lots of grass. It's almost the country. There are people sitting or lying on the grass, children running. Youngsters tearing down the slopes on bicycles.

The father and his child climb up the highest hill. It's hard for the child. When she tires, her father puts her on his shoulders. From up there the child risks this gesture, wrapping her arms around her father's neck. She presses her cheek to her father's head and is happy to be reacquainted with the smell of his hair, and of his skin, which is always mingled with the smell of pipe tobacco.

They reach the summit. Hoisted up on her father's shoulders, the child feels she's on top of the world.

Above them and around them there's nothing but the vast blue sky, dangling its unusual-shaped clouds over the city, a city they can see stretching away in the distance, hazy, unreal-looking. It's the clouds that look real, these big, cottony, slow-moving clouds depicting things up there, an ocean, waves, cliffs. Everything else has stopped existing.

'Look, my darling,' says the father, 'look how pretty it is… That's what the sea looks like, you know.'

But what the child heard, the important thing she's just heard, something she's more interested in than the sea, which she's never seen, is that her father called her *my darling*. For the first time he spoke to her the way her mother used to. And he called her, the child, the name he used to call her mother.

The child's heart starts beating faster. Now's the time to do it. She's going to put the unspoken question to him. She's going to ask him. Now.

She does it in a very quiet voice, a voice so quiet you might wonder whether he'll hear.

'Daddy, are you going to come back home?'

But he has, he has heard her, and he heard so clearly you'd think he'd been stung by a wasp.

He peels the child's little arms away from his neck and sets her gently down on the ground. And then, very bluntly, very clearly, he says, 'France, you know very well that's impossible.'

It's true, she knows perfectly well. The child realizes she knows this. She knew it.

They set off down the hill hand in hand. The father talks about one thing and another, in a smiling voice.

Near the bus stop there's a man selling candyfloss. The father buys a big stick of it for the child.

On the journey back, hiding behind the pink cloud she's nibbling her way through, the child thinks things over.

She understands so much now.

Perhaps it's that evening, the evening of the fortifications, perhaps it's the evening of another Sunday spent with her father, but it is a Sunday because the intermittent sounds of a street party can be heard wafting outside. The child has her own key now, and the father uses it to open the door for her before slipping away, never once coming in. When she gets inside, the child calls her mother. She doesn't see her straight away. Then she finds her all alone, sitting in the kitchen. The light isn't on and it's already dark.

The mother's alone, sitting on a stool, motionless. The child sees her from behind. And, hearing a noise, the mother turns round. The child notices she's still in her dressing gown, as she was this morning, when the child left. She must have spent the day like this, in the kitchen. She looks so lost, so miserable, that the child is quite struck by it. As if seeing her in this condition for the first time. Although it's not the first time. But it's the first time the child notices it.

Is it because the mother's sitting on a low stool that the child suddenly thinks she looks very small? She even feels that she, the child, is bigger than her. It feels, oddly, as if the roles have been reversed, as if the mother has become the child and the child the mother.

She goes over to her mother, who has turned away from her again, and affectionately, as she used to before, she puts her arms around her neck. And when the mother, in her surprise, turns imperceptibly to look at her, the child delves her small fingers into her black hair and, quite naturally, so naturally, asks, 'Do you want me to brush your hair, Mummy?'

And, in that position, standing behind her mother, she really is bigger now.

This evening, the two of them are back in this kitchen, alone, as if nothing has gone on, as if nothing has happened. As if no one knows the father.

Everything's almost like the old days.

But there's that music, the music from the party outside, which tells them the war's over. That time has passed. That the child has indeed grown bigger.

One morning, looking out of the kitchen window, the child watches the concierge playing with his daughter in the courtyard. This girl is just a little older than the child. In her hair she's wearing a big blue bow, which the child envies. But the mother thinks it looks a bit 'Easter egg' and doesn't want to buy her one. The concierge's daughter is throwing a little red ball to her father and he catches it cack-handedly. He's a hefty, dark-haired man who came home from the war in the last convoy of prisoners.

The concierge's daughter is laughing because her father makes such a funny face as he tries to catch the little ball in his big hands. The concierge is actually so clumsy only because he's watching his daughter more than the ball. He has that gleam of admiration and tenderness that the child has occasionally seen in her father's eye. And then, in a flash, when he's missed the ball yet again, he throws himself at his daughter, picks her up in his arms, way up high, and spins her around with him. She shrieks with mock terror and delight.

The child closes the window.

That same feeling when, in the street, now, while she's doing the shopping with her mother, she comes across a father holding his child's hand, walking at his child's pace and leaning down to talk to him or her.

The child's father won't be coming back. He's really left. For ever. He's no longer part of this household, the child's and her mother's household. She now knows that. She understands it. Far more fully, more quickly, than her mother, who still cries from time to time, but it's hard to know exactly why.

These separations, it turns out, have a name: divorce. The child learns this word. And its derivatives. The father and mother are divorced. The mother is a divorcee. What about me, am I a divorcee? asks the child. No, she's told, not at all, what a thought! That child really is a fool, says the grandmother. And yet the child herself feels very divorced.

But she doesn't cry, not her. It's just that, despite her new and extensive understanding of things, she's become a little deaf, a little blind to the world around her. It's as if, with her degree of understanding, she's lost some of her curiosity about it.

She understands perfectly that her father has become the husband of another woman, the blonde lady whose name is Agnès.

She understands that they live in their own apartment, where she's invited to spend the day on a Sunday from time to time.

She understands that this couple soon have a baby – a real one this time, which won't be dismissed as a dream. A baby her father will hold in his big freckled hands, whose smell and warmth the child is gradually forgetting.

She understands that this little boy will call her father Daddy.

She'll even understand that one day this little boy will be astonished to hear her calling his father Daddy.

She understands everything, and this everything, she believes, means nothing to her.

That's how one day you stop being a child and you end up calling yourself France, like everyone else.

Over the years of apprenticeship, when the child and her father see each other, they will each keep to their roles and they'll play them as they should be played, as they're both expected to play them. And yet they will sometimes recognize each other, the father and the child, for a moment, just like that, a stolen moment, in the middle of other people's conversations, cutting across the presence of others. They'll find each other.

They look at each other, and it's no longer France that he sees, but his child. And for her, it's not the husband of the blonde lady, but her father, her own father. The man who was her father for a short time. Such a short time.

And in that eye contact there is a lot of sadness, and a bit of happiness. But this, well, this is their secret.

Images from the past, so distant, so fragmentary, that they seem rather laughable.

The child has become a grown-up. She's a woman. It's a long time now since she laid bare her parents' secrets. Found out about it all, analysed, understood and swept it aside.

She has hushed the child she once was. Has reduced her to silence, to an indulgent oblivion, a smile.

France has wrung the child's neck. Has made her forget the furious love she once felt for a second-hand father.

The father and daughter live in different cities, far apart. They both lead full lives. See each other once a year, perhaps. Sometimes less. There are telephone calls. Conversations about this and that, family events, work, health. Glossing lightly over things.

About nothing. These conversations are about nothing.

No proper conversations were ever had.

Nothing was ever said.

She still likes calling her father, though. It's always him who picks up. Hello. She hears his voice. The voice from before. The voice from the old days. 'Hello, Daddy?' she says, and then, just for a second, it's as if anything could happen. One second. But nothing happens. She says only the expected things. He does the same probably. Never anything real. Never anything that matters. Nothing of what matters to her. In fact she only ever calls when everything's going well, when she can give a positive image of herself. Of his life, she never asks anything. She doesn't actually know anything. She's never known anything. She'll never know anything. Perhaps she doesn't want to know anything.

But every now and then, lurking beneath particular words, beneath an inflection in a voice, on one end of the line or the other, there's something more, the beginnings of something, a sort of complicity. Nothing is said, though. Ever.

One evening, it's not him who answers the telephone. She's told that her father has just died. Then she realizes it's too late. That they'll never talk.

No emotion. She doesn't cry. It doesn't feel real.

So, she thinks simply, I didn't see him again. She didn't have time. Which doesn't mean anything.

She attends the funeral as if in a dream, without a tear.

This death, the reality of this death, will hit her a few weeks later.

It is when she comes home from a dinner, she's had a little too much to drink, she feels good, happy, she suddenly feels like calling her father and telling him so, just like that. She has, monstrously, forgotten he's dead. But in the time it takes to start reaching for the telephone she remembers, and her hand drops back.

She remembers, and it is only then that she realizes her father is dead. That she understands it.

She understands she'll never be able to call him again. She'll never talk to him again. Never hear him again. Never again hear that voice.

And it's now too late to understand each other.

As for his giraffe-hands, he'll never know.

That's when her grief begins.

And then one day, much later, something strange happens.

She's travelling back to Paris after a long trip, the train's packed. She's tired, a bit sad. Alone. She knows there's no one waiting for her.

They're approaching Gare de l'Est and she's got up from her seat to stand by the door, wanting to get onto the platform as quickly as possible, to avoid the crush. She's standing in that cramped space where there are several other impatient passengers facing away from each other, motionless, their eyes pinned on the windows in the door, looking for signs of the station in the darkness, switched off from anything else, indifferent to each other. She too is switched off, indifferent, filled with the boredom and weariness of this homeward journey.

When all at once something catches her eye, draws all her attention, something surprising and yet familiar, an isolated image which gives her an incomprehensible, violent blast of emotion: right in front of her, on a level with her eyes, is another passenger's hand, just his hand, in a raincoat; she can't see the rest of him.

A hand clasping the rail to the right of the door. This hand is quite old, quite rough, big, with very white skin, covered with rusty freckles, a hand she would recognize in a thousand. A hand which must smell of tobacco and eau de cologne, she knows that, a hand which is both strong and gentle.

And then and there, the child, miraculously herself once more, remembers so exactly the smell of that hand, its gentleness, and the furious intensity of her child's love that her heart beats very hard. She suddenly has such a desperate longing to touch that hand, she could almost cry, to touch it, kiss it, take refuge in it.

A vertiginous wave of tenderness which lasts only a moment.

They've arrived. The man in the raincoat drops his hand, turns round before stepping onto the platform: the false likeness of her father evaporates.

But the true one now lives on in the child. For good.

No one will notice the young woman's eyes are full of tears. Of happiness. Of sheer gratitude.

Subscribe

Peirene Press publishes series of world-class contemporary novellas. An annual subscription consists of three books chosen from across the world connected by a single theme.

The books will be sent out in December (in time for Christmas), May and September. Any title in the series already in print when you order will be posted immediately.

The perfect way for book lovers to collect all the Peirene titles.

> *'A class act.'* GUARDIAN

> *'Two-hour books to be devoured in a single sitting: literary cinema for those fatigued by film.'* TLS

£35   1 Year Subscription (3 books, free p&p)

£65   2 Year Subscription (6 books, free p&p)

£90   3 Year Subscription (9 books, free p&p)

Peirene Press, 17 Cheverton Road, London N19 3BB
T 020 7686 1941
E subscriptions@peirenepress.com

www.peirenepress.com/shop
with secure online ordering facility

Peirene's Series

COMING-OF-AGE: TOWARDS IDENTITY

NO 13
The Dead Lake by Hamid Ismailov
Translated from the Russian by Andrew Bromfield
'Immense poetic power.' GUARDIAN

NO 14
The Blue Room by Hanne Ørstavik
Translated from the Norwegian by Deborah Dawkin
'Shrewd and psychologically adroit.' LANCASHIRE
EVENING POST

NO 15
Under the Tripoli Sky by Kamal Ben Hameda
Translated from the French by Adriana Hunter
'It is excellent.' SUNDAY TIMES

....
CHANCE ENCOUNTER: MEETING THE OTHER

NO 16
White Hunger by Aki Ollikainen
Translated from the Finnish by Emily Jeremiah and Fleur Jeremiah
'A tale of epic substance.'
LOS ANGELES REVIEW OF BOOKS

NO 17
Reader for Hire by Raymond Jean
Translated from the French by Adriana Hunter
'A book that will make you want to read more books.'
COSMOPOLITAN

NO 18
The Looking-Glass Sisters by Gøhril Gabrielsen
Translated from the Norwegian by John Irons
'Disturbs and challenges.' THE NATIONAL

COUNTERPOINTS ARTS

Peirene Press is proud to support Counterpoints Arts.

Counterpoints Arts is a charity that promotes the creative arts by and about refugees and migrants in the UK.

'We are living in a time of human displacement. We need bold and imaginative interventions to help us make sense of migration. And who better to do this than artists who are engaging with this issue.'

ALMIR KOLDZIC AND ÁINE O'BRIEN, DIRECTORS, COUNTERPOINTS ARTS

By buying this book you are helping Counterpoints Arts enhance the cultural integration of refugees – a mission which will surely change our society for the better.

Peirene will donate 50p from the sale of this book to the charity.

www.counterpointsarts.org.uk